"You're going to be a father."

"Don't use that word," Nick said sharply. "I can't be a father."

"In about six months, you will be."

"No, I won't." He dropped onto the edge of his desk. "I can't do this, Sierra. Won't do it. This is the last thing I ever wanted."

"You don't have a choice, Nick." It was hard to speak over the ache in her chest. "It's reality."

"I don't want children. I don't even want to think about children." He stared at her, his eyes dark with panic. Denial. "A kid would ruin my life."

Dear Reader,

What would you do if your entire world suddenly crumbled?

When Sierra Clark receives devastating news, it's her boss, Nick Boone, who finds her, who tries to comfort her, who holds her as she cries. But comfort turns into something else entirely, and neither of them is prepared for the consequences.

No one wants to think about getting that phone call, the one that changes everything. Since I love my characters, it was hard to start this book by dealing my heroine such a devastating loss. But I enjoyed discovering how Nick and Sierra coped with impending parenthood, and how each of them had to change in order to become a couple. Like the rest of us, they had an inner strength, and they needed every bit of it to resolve their problems.

Sometimes, it's the things we thought we'd never want that turn out to be exactly what we were looking for all along.

I love to hear from my readers. Contact me at margaret@margaretwatson.com, or visit my website, www.margaretwatson.com.

Margaret Watson

For Baby and Me
Margaret Watson

™
Harlequin®

TORONTO NEW YORK LONDON
AMSTERDAM PARIS SYDNEY HAMBURG
STOCKHOLM ATHENS TOKYO MILAN MADRID
PRAGUE WARSAW BUDAPEST AUCKLAND

Recycling programs for this product may not exist in your area.

ISBN-13: 978-0-373-71696-8

FOR BABY AND ME

ABOUT THE AUTHOR

Margaret Watson has always made up stories in her head. When she started actually writing them down, she realized she'd found exactly what she wanted to do with the rest of her life. Almost twenty years after staring at that first blank page, she's an award-winning, two-time RITA® Award finalist who was recently honored by Harlequin for her twenty-fifth book.

Margaret spends as much time as possible visiting the area that inspires her books, the Door County, Wisconsin, cities of Algoma and Sturgeon Bay. When she's not eating Door County cherries, smoked fish and cheese, she lives in a Chicago suburb with her husband and three daughters and a menagerie of pets.

Books by Margaret Watson

HARLEQUIN SUPERROMANCE

1205—TWO ON THE RUN
1258—HOMETOWN GIRL
1288—IN HER DEFENSE
1337—FAMILY FIRST
1371—SMALL-TOWN SECRETS
1420—SMALL-TOWN FAMILY
1508—A PLACE CALLED HOME*
1531—NO PLACE LIKE HOME*
1554—HOME AT LAST*
1608—AN UNLIKELY SETUP
1638—CAN'T STAND THE HEAT?
1673—LIFE REWRITTEN

*The McInnes Triplets

For Bill,
always my hero.

CHAPTER ONE

"HOLD ON. I CAN'T HEAR you."

Pressing the phone to her ear, Sierra wove through the cocktail party crowd, straining to hear above the noise.

Rain sheeted down on the small balcony as she stepped out through the sliding glass door. Shivering, she pressed herself flat beneath the overhang and pulled the door closed. The wind whistled over the faint hum of cars from the street below, but it felt like silence after the chatter of the party.

"Okay. I'm good now. Can you start over?"

"Is this Sierra Clark?"

"Yes, it is." Was this a client? She didn't recognize the voice. "Who is this?"

"Ms. Clark, this is Sheriff Kurt Allen of Barber County, Colorado. Are you the daughter of Delbert and Eleanor Clark of Wilmette, Illinois?"

Her heart lurched. "Yes, they're my parents." Her fingers dug into her cell phone. "Why are you calling me?"

"Ms. Clark, I have some bad news." The sheriff

cleared his throat. "Your parents were killed in a plane crash earlier this evening."

Cold rain battered her face and needled through her silk shirt. "What?" The frigid air was too heavy to breathe. "My parents? Colorado? That can't be right." She stared at the Los Angeles skyline, blurred by the rain.

"I'm sorry." His voice softened. "The small plane was identified as belonging to Delbert Clark. Identification on the bodies indicates he and Eleanor Clark were the victims."

Victims? Bodies? Mom and Dad? "No. No, that's not possible." She wrapped her arm around her waist. "They're not in Colorado. They're in Wilmette. At home. There's been a mistake." Someone else was supposed to get this phone call. She'd hang up, dial her parents and hear their voices. Then she could breathe again.

"I'm sorry, Ms. Clark." The sympathy in the man's voice made her want to throw the phone off the balcony. "There's no mistake. Perhaps you'll want to contact the rest of your family. You can call us back when you're ready to make the arrangements." He gave her a number and the line went dead. He'd hung up.

Cold raindrops pelted her face and chest, and tiny pinpricks of pain burrowed deep inside her. Her hands shaking, she pressed the speed dial for her parents' home. It rang and rang, but no one answered.

She tried her father's cell, then her mother's. Not even a dial tone. They both went straight to voice mail. Sierra's hair fell over her face, the curls dripping water down her cheeks, channeling tears onto her chest. The phone scraped against her ear as she listened to first her father, then her mother, tell her to leave a message.

As she ended the calls, she saw the red light blinking and the text box on the screen. "You have one new voice message." Her parents' phone number.

Fingers fumbling, she retrieved the voice mail.

"Hey, honey." Her mom's voice. Happy. Carefree. "Dad and I are off to Colorado for the weekend. Suzie lent us her condo in Aspen. I'll call you when we get home."

"No!" The scream disappeared into the wind and rain. Just like her parents.

The glass at her back was slippery as she sank to the cold concrete surface of the balcony. Water soaked her skirt, drenched her blouse, numbed her feet in their strappy heels. When the cheery voice asked if she wanted to save or delete this voice mail, she covered her head with her arms against the slicing rain.

Hey, honey. Dad and I are off to Colorado. Off to Colorado. Off to Colorado.

"Sierra?"

The voice came from far away. She barely heard it, didn't bother to look up. Nothing anyone could say was important.

"Sierra?" A hand brushed her shoulder. "What's wrong?"

She turned her head slowly. Nick Boone, her boss, was crouched next to her, rain splattering his dark suit jacket.

"You're soaking wet." He tugged at her arm. "You should come inside where it's warm."

"Doesn't matter." She closed her eyes as the rain soaked her hair, ran in rivulets down the back of her neck. She would never be warm again.

"Sierra!" He put his arm around her waist and lifted her. "What's wrong? Did you have too much to drink?"

He had her on her feet, but she was swaying. Her teeth chattered and her body shook. The blouse dripped water down her arms, onto her fingers, onto the concrete. Onto Nick's shoes. The light from the balcony reflected off them.

He shrugged off his suit jacket and slung it around her shoulders, then opened the door, releasing a blast of warm air. She tried to walk, but her feet wouldn't work.

Nick wrapped his arm around her waist and steered her into the crowded, noisy room. Voices pounded in her ears, bodies jostled her, but they were all a blur. She read shock on someone's face. Pity in another's. How did they know?

"You're drenched," Nick said as he walked her toward the exit. "How long were you out there?"

How long does it take for a world to crumble? "Forever."

"Sierra, what's going on?" His arm tightened around her waist. "For God's sake, this is a professional conference. You have to be careful." He peered at her face, then grabbed both her arms. She swayed once more, and his hands tightened. "Did someone put something in your drink?"

The smell of seafood, salty and pungent, drifted past, along with the tang of lemon. Her stomach churned.

"Sierra? What were you…?" Nick's voice became part of the noise around her.

A moment later he leaned closer, and she smelled the scotch he'd been drinking. Scotch. What her father drank. She closed her eyes.

Nick pulled her against his side, close enough that she could feel the rise and fall of his chest. The rhythm of his breathing.

He felt as warm as a furnace, and she tried to get even nearer. The cold was eating her alive. Consuming every inch of her.

As she shook, his jacket began to slide off her shoulders. He pulled it around her with his other hand, bundling her into a cocoon, trapping in the cold. The smell of wet wool washed over her.

"Sierra?" He bent his head to hers, and his breath feathered through the wet hair over her ear. "Can you walk?"

She took a step, then another. The noise of the party pounded at her, fading as they moved through a doorway. Cool air rippled over her wet blouse, making her shake more violently.

"If I let you go, can you stand?" Nick's voice again.

She nodded.

He bent and started removing her high heels. His

hands were hot on the bare skin of her ankle as he slipped the strap off the back and eased one sandal off. As he removed the other shoe, his palm curved over her calf.

Nick guided her into a small alcove and onto a stone bench. It chilled the backs of her thighs as she sat, and she hunched her shoulders.

"Are you sick?"

His blue eyes studied her face, and she forced herself to focus on him, the man she'd been working with for almost three years. She'd been nothing but professional with him. Always calm, always prepared, always exacting in her work. No drama, no scenes.

Why did Nick have to be the one who found her? Why did he have to be the witness to her disintegration?

She wanted to get up and run away. Hide. Bury herself in a hole and block out everything else. But he still had his arm around her. Holding her in place. Preventing her escape.

She licked her lips, which felt dry and chapped. How could they, when the rest of her was so wet? "I…I got a phone call. My parents were killed in a plane crash."

He stared at her for a moment, then she saw understanding sweep over his face. He sucked in a breath. "Oh my God."

He opened the cocktail purse at her wrist and rummaged inside. Pulled out her hotel key. "What's your room number?"

She stared at him blankly.

"Sierra." His face came close again. His eyes were

the color of the sky. Had her parents seen that color before they died?

Nick shook her gently. "What room are you staying in?"

She stared at him blankly, and he pushed her wet hair out of her face and tucked it behind her ear. "What room are you in, Sierra?"

She closed her eyes. "Fifteen something. No. Twelve."

"Okay." He pulled her upright and she stumbled with him to the elevator, his arm steady around her. His fingers pressed tight above her hip; his palm rested in the curve of her waist.

A bland, horrible version of a Beatles song played. "I Get By With a Little Help from my Friends." She stared at the elevator door. The metallic surface reflected a stranger's white face, streaks of mascara on her cheeks. Nick held her shoes in one hand, supporting her with the other. She began to cry.

A soft ping and the door opened. The lighting in the corridor was muted, the carpet thick and sound absorbing. That was good. Sierra couldn't stop crying.

"Do you remember your room number?" Nick's voice was soft. Understanding. She'd rather he remain the brusque man from the balcony. The one who'd thought she was drunk.

The kindness in his voice made the tears fall faster.

Her room. "Fifteen. Twelve fifteen. Magna Carta."

He paused in the door of the elevator. "You remembered your room number because of the year the Magna Carta was signed."

"Twelve fifteen. Yes."

"A woman with hidden depths." He curled his arm around her waist again and led her down the hall. When they reached her room, he let her go carefully and unlocked the door.

Inside, the room smelled like disinfectant overlaid with cloying air freshener. He put her shoes in the closet, then took her arms.

"Do you have brothers or sisters? Can I dial them for you?"

"No." She felt his jacket slip off her shoulders and whisper past her legs as it landed on the floor. Cool air from the vent above the bed washed over her, and she shivered. "Th-thank you. No brothers or sisters." No family, other than a distant aunt and uncle.

She was an orphan now.

Sinking onto the bed, she drew her knees to her chest and let the tears fall.

Nick was still there, at the end of the bed. She stared at the bedspread, a blinding white duvet. "Thank you for walking me up here," she said, her voice thick and hoarse. Why wouldn't he leave and let her fall apart?

Another long moment stretched as she struggled to control herself. "Sierra, I can't leave you alone after news like this. You need to get warmed up. Why don't you take a shower?"

"I'm fine," she said.

"You're not fine." His voice was more gentle than she ever imagined it could be. "You're in shock. Freezing cold. You need to warm up."

Warm. Yes. She needed to be warm.

"Okay." She slid off the bed, then stood there, swaying.

He reached around her, the sleeve of his blue cotton dress shirt brushing her cheek, and unfastened her lapis necklace. The one her mother had given her to celebrate her first architectural job. The start of her career.

Nick stared at her, as if waiting for her to do something. Finally, he put his hand on her back and guided her toward the bathroom. "Take a shower, Sierra. Warm up. I'll wait. You shouldn't be alone right now."

Alone. That's what she was. What she would be from now on.

He left the bathroom door ajar behind her. She began to undress, but the tiny pearl buttons down the front of her blouse seemed to have gotten much bigger. She fumbled as she tried to push them through the tiny holes.

"Sierra?" Nick cracked the door open and peered in. "Do you need help?"

She looked down at the blouse. "No." She fumbled with the buttons again, but couldn't manage to undo them. Finally, he stepped in, moved her hands away and unbuttoned the blouse. It fell open, revealing her cream-colored bra. The lacy one she'd chosen to go with the blouse.

He slid his hands to the waistband of her skirt. They were trembling as he unhooked, then unzipped the garment. It slid off her hips and landed on the floor in a dark blue puddle. "You can do the rest, can't you?"

His voice sounded rusty. She nodded.

He backed out of the room, and this time the door clicked shut. She turned on the shower, waiting until it was hot, and stepped in.

Sierra stood under the spray, feeling it cascade over her body, and thought about her mom and dad. Had they suffered? Had they known they were going to die?

She sank to the floor of the shower, curled into a ball and sobbed.

NICK STOOD AT THE BATHROOM door, listening to the water beat down. Listening to Sierra cry. She'd been crying for fifteen minutes.

He cracked the door, and steam billowed out. "Sierra? Are you okay?"

Nothing. He'd have to check on her.

He didn't want to see her naked. Having to undress her was bad enough. Seeing all that pale skin and her long legs, the purple string bikini, the creamy lace of her bra, had rattled him. Made him want.

He was a bastard.

Steam filled the shower, leaving her a smudgy figure curled on the tiled floor. Her head was on her knees and her red hair, long and dark, hung around her face. Her body shook with sobs.

"Sierra. You need to get out of the shower." When she didn't respond, he said more loudly, "Turn off the water."

She stared at him as if she had no idea who he was. He grabbed the hotel's bulky terry cloth bathrobe off the door hook and held it in front of him like a shield, high enough that he could see only her face. "Come on, Sierra." *Please, God, don't make me pull her out of that shower.*

"Nick." She frowned, then glanced at the robe he held. "It's warm in here."

"It'll be warm out there, too. I turned up the heat."

Her hair hung in twisted ropes around her shoulders. She blinked, then stood up as he hastily raised the robe. She slapped at the fixture a couple of times before the water finally stopped.

She stepped into his arms.

Closing his eyes, Nick wrapped the robe around her body. It fell to her ankles, and he could have wrapped it around her twice. She struggled to push her arms into the sleeves, then fumbled for the sash at her waist.

When she turned to face him, the deep V of the robe plunged down between her breasts. He tugged the lapels together and pulled the sash tighter. Then he grabbed a towel and laid it over her shoulder. "Why don't you dry your hair? I don't…I don't know how to do that."

It was too intimate. Far more intimate than holding the robe while she got out of the shower.

She leaned forward and rubbed her hair. When she dropped the towel onto the floor, the strands were curly. He'd never seen her with curls. As his gaze slid down her face to her throat and that V of skin, he pulled the lapels tight again.

He steered her into the room, his hand at her back.

Her skin was warm through the robe, and her feet were red from the hot water.

She stood in the middle of the room and stared out the window at the lights of Los Angeles. How would it feel to get that kind of phone call? He had no idea.

He opened the small refrigerator and pulled out a bottle of water. "Drink this," he said. She'd cried so many tears, she was probably dehydrated.

She cracked off the cap and drank deeply. When she had drained the bottle, she walked to the hotel desk and opened her laptop.

By the time he reached her, she'd connected to the internet and was searching *plane crash Barber County Colorado.*

He took her hands away and held them in one of his, then closed the lid. "You don't want to do that."

"I need to know. I have to find out what happened."

"Later. Not right now."

He drew her slowly against him, bracing himself for the contact. For the feel of her body next to his. "They're gone," he said softly. "Nothing you can read or see is going to change that. Is it going to make you feel better to view the wreckage of their plane?"

At those words, she collapsed against him and began to sob again. He hesitated, then pulled her close. Her head fitted into the crook of his neck, and her tears dripped onto his shoulder. Her hair smelled like the hotel shampoo.

She curled her arms around his neck and sagged

against him, crying. Ragged sounds of pain came from her throat, and he half carried, half led her to the bed. He sank down, pulling her onto his lap. She burrowed into him. "Stay, please," she whispered.

"I'll stay." He brushed her damp hair away from her face and pulled it out of the neck of her robe. "I'll stay as long as you want."

Her white-clad body bowed with pain as she clung to him. He didn't want to stay. He didn't want to see her raw grief, her shock. His feet shifted restlessly on the floor and his hands fluttered helplessly. How the hell was he supposed to comfort her?

A number of the women he'd dated had called him heartless, and they were right. But even *he* couldn't leave her alone, crying, in a hotel room two thousand miles from her home, back in Chicago.

Nick's hand caught in her dark red curls as he stroked her head. Curly strands twined around his fingers like ivy searching for an anchor. She'd pressed her face against his shoulder, and her chest rose and fell with her sobs.

His mother had been gone for more than twenty years. He'd cried, too, when she'd disappeared, shortly after his twelfth birthday.

After he'd gone into the system, he hadn't cried again.

With a final sniffle, Sierra eased away from him and reached for the box of tissues on the nightstand. Her robe gaped open, and he caught a glimpse of her nipple, a dark shadow against her pale skin. It puckered as cool air washed over it.

Nick closed his eyes, but it was too late. He stirred beneath her. When she settled back against him and rubbed her cheek against his chest, he hardened.

"Are you…are you okay by yourself now?" he asked, desperate to leave.

"I'm sorry." She jumped up and swayed on her feet. "You had plans tonight. I'm fine. Thank you."

She clearly wasn't fine. "I don't have plans. I thought you'd want to be by yourself."

She stared out the window again as her eyes swam with tears. "By myself. Yes." Her voice was so soft he barely heard her. "I am."

Feeling helpless, he awkwardly pulled her into another hug. Her arms went around his neck and clung.

As he stroked her back, she pressed closer. He shut his eyes and tried to think about the specs for the building he was currently designing, the workshop he was leading tomorrow, the projects waiting for him back in Chicago. Nothing helped. His erection grew harder as it pressed into her abdomen.

Sierra stilled in his arms and lifted her head from his chest. "Nick?" She looked confused. Bewildered.

"I'm sorry, Sierra." His face heated and he tried to set her away, but her arms tightened around his neck.

She stared at him for a long moment, then rose on tiptoe and pressed her mouth to his.

Her tears were salty on her lips, and her mouth trembled. He tried to stay perfectly still, but couldn't help responding when she licked his lips.

He tried to keep the kiss gentle. Comforting instead of erotic. But she pressed her breasts against his chest, and a vision of her nipple filled his head.

Heat built between them, until she was clutching at his hair. She opened her mouth, and he tasted the wine she'd drunk at the reception.

"Stay with me, Nick," she whispered.

"That would be a very bad idea." He tried to put her away from him, but his hands wouldn't let her go.

"I need to feel something besides pain. Besides loss. I need to know I'm alive." She fused her mouth to his and kissed him with awkward urgency. Her body trembled again, but this time, it wasn't with cold. "Stay," she murmured against his lips.

"An honorable man would walk away, Sierra. Right now." He'd been called a bastard more times than he could count, but even he had limits.

Without taking her mouth from his, she shook her head. "Please. I need…I need you. I need to *feel*."

She pulled his shirt from his waistband and ran her hands up his back. Down to his hips. He groaned and framed her face with his hands. "You don't know what you're asking," he said. His hands trembled on her skin. "You're upset. Confused. You'll regret this in the morning."

"No regrets." Her fingers fumbled with his belt. The bathrobe slipped down her arms, exposing her breasts, her abdomen. Her nipples were hard and tight, and her chest was flushed. When he heard the rasp of his belt as she pulled it off, he pushed the robe to the floor and stepped out of his slacks.

He trembled as he touched her, as she touched him. Without breaking their kiss, he reached for his wallet and fumbled for the condom he kept there. She wanted to forget, and he'd do that for her. He was good at making women forget.

When he eased her onto to the bed, she rose to meet him. When she shattered, he held her tightly as he joined her. When he drew away, she turned into his shoulder and fell asleep. Her tears burned like acid as they fell onto his skin.

SIERRA WOKE WHEN HER DOOR clicked shut. It was still dark—3:00 a.m. He was gone.

She remembered why he'd been here, and her heart clenched tight. *Mom. Dad.*

She curled into a ball beneath the duvet, staring at the shadows on the wall. Finally, she picked up the phone and called the airline.

"I have a family emergency. I need to go home."

CHAPTER TWO

SIERRA STARED AT THE pink line down the center of the screen on the plastic stick, and her stomach churned. Dropping the stick, she bent over the toilet again and retched. But there was nothing left in her stomach.

She slid to the floor and leaned against the wall, dizzy and weak. The heat vent beneath her channeled warm air up her back, taking away the chill. The white stick lay next to her on the slate-tiled floor, the pink even brighter than the test she'd taken yesterday.

She couldn't be pregnant. She'd had sex once in the past year. That night. With Nick.

He'd worn a condom.

But the stick had turned pink three days in a row.

Her hand curled over her abdomen as she struggled to stand. She needed her mother. Her mom would have hugged her and told her it was going to be okay. That they would figure it out together.

Sierra turned on the shower and dropped her boxers and T-shirt on the floor. She'd have to figure this out on her own.

A half hour later, chewing on a cracker, she got on the El and watched as the skyscrapers in the Loop grew closer. The earbuds of her iPod played Billy Joel as the train swayed from side to side, and she closed her eyes to prevent the tears from falling. She and her dad had gone to his concert in Wrigley Field the summer before, the one with Elton John. Her dad had been so excited that she liked *his* music.

She yanked the buds out of her ear, turned off her iPod and stuffed it into her briefcase.

When she reached the Loop, she joined the throngs of people pouring into her building, and waited in line for an elevator. Ahead of her, a dark head was visible above the crowd. Nick. Even from the back, she knew it was him.

He stepped onto an elevator, his arm over the shoulder of a blonde woman in a business suit. She smiled up at him, sleek and feline, and Sierra looked away.

She'd seen Nick with a different woman the week before. She'd met her friend Callie for dinner, and Nick had walked past the restaurant with a stunning redhead. Two weeks before that, a different blonde had shown up at the firm, gone into his office and shut the door.

Sierra's stomach churned as she waited for the elevator to close, then got on the next one. What if she really was pregnant? What if the test hadn't been some sort of mistake?

If she was pregnant, Nick Boone, the ultimate player, was the father of her baby.

The crackers in her stomach were suddenly as heavy as bricks. He couldn't commit to a woman for longer than a week or two. How could he have a child?

She pulled out her phone and texted Callie: Meet after work?

There was no sign of the blonde in the office. Nick's door was open as Sierra walked past, and she couldn't stop herself from glancing inside.

He looked up just as she did, and stilled for a moment. Then he smiled. "Good morning, Sierra."

"Hey, Nick." She smiled just as casually. Neither one of them had mentioned that night in Los Angeles. Nick had come to her parents' funeral, along with everyone else from the office. He'd hugged her, being careful to tilt his body away from hers. And when she'd returned to work, he'd told her to take as much time off as she needed. Asked if there was anything the company could do for her.

During the conversation, he'd looked at her hands, her mouth, her throat. Everywhere but her eyes.

He clearly didn't want to discuss the night in Los Angeles, which was fine with her. She wanted to bury everything about that night so deep in her memory that it would never resurface. But the pink line on the stick this morning made that impossible. What had happened that night was going to change the rest of her life.

And Nick's.

NICK LISTENED TO THE sound of Sierra's footsteps fading as she headed toward her office, then turned his attention to the papers on his desk. He didn't see them, though. All he saw was Sierra in a white bathrobe, her wet hair curling over her shoulders, devastation in her eyes.

He'd revisited that night far too often. Called himself every name in the book for what he'd done.

Then relived it in his dreams.

When they talked or worked together, she was nothing but professional. But her guard was up. There was a stiffness in her shoulders that hadn't been there before.

She hadn't said one word to him about that night, though. Apparently, she wanted to pretend that the fumbling, awkward sex hadn't happened.

That was exactly what he should do, too. He shouldn't have touched her. The moment she'd leaned forward on his lap, he should have walked out of the room.

But he hadn't.

And now he had to remember, every time he saw her.

The anguish in her eyes. The vulnerability. Her tears, soaking into his shirt.

The feel of her body beneath his.

The uncomfortable, impossible-to-shake guilt that had dogged him ever since.

Even worse, the selfish regret. By staying with her that night, he'd shut the door on any future relationship with her.

She'd fascinated him from the day she walked in for an interview. It had taken him about five minutes to know he would hire her.

Ten minutes to know he wanted her.

Fifteen to know she wasn't the kind of woman he got involved with. He wanted a good time and no strings. She was all about the white picket fence and happily ever after. If he hadn't known it before, it had slapped him in the face at her parents' funeral.

The happy pictures of the three of them together were, for him, like snapshots of a puzzling, foreign civilization. Sierra and her parents had always been touching each other. Hugging. Smiling and laughing. Looking at those pictures, he found it impossible not to see the love they'd shared.

He didn't do love. He didn't even do strong like.

He didn't get involved with women like Sierra.

Now, the best he could hope for was that the guilt would eventually fade. That they'd be easy with one another. Friendly. It would never be the same—it never was, once you got naked with a woman. He usually didn't regret that, but he regretted it with Sierra.

His phone rang, and he grabbed it. He needed a distraction from his thoughts. "Yes, Janet?"

"Walker Barnes is here, Nick."

"Great. Put him in the conference room and get him some coffee. I'll be right there."

He'd designed Barnes's office space in the Loop. Now the CEO of GeekBoy was interested in a house. Nick had forgotten about the appointment, or he would have talked to Sierra already.

Her head was bent over her keyboard when he knocked on her door. She swiveled in her chair. "Nick. Come in."

He'd surprised her. If he hadn't, he never would have seen that momentary vulnerability in her eyes. She banished it almost immediately, but not quickly enough. For a moment, that night in Los Angeles hovered between them. Her dark red hair fell in a neat braid down her back, but he remembered the curls sliding between his fingers like ropes of silk. She wore a blue suit today with a plain blouse. But he remembered how she'd looked when that robe had fallen to the floor.

Clearing his throat, he dropped into the chair next to her desk. "Do you remember Walker Barnes? We designed the office space for his company, GeekBoy. You had just started with us."

"I do remember that." Her fingers uncurled from the mouse, relaxed. Had she thought he was going to bring up that night?

"He wants us to design a house for him. Since home design is becoming your specialty, do you want to take the lead on the preplanning conference?"

"I'd love to." She drew a pad of paper out of a drawer. "What, in general, is he looking for? And when are we going to meet with him?"

"He's here now, in the conference room."

She grabbed a pencil and stood up. "Then let's not keep him waiting."

Nick waited for Sierra to precede him out the door, putting one hand lightly on her back. Her muscles tensed beneath his fingers, and he thought he heard her breath hitch. Then she stepped away and didn't look back as she headed down the hall.

His admin stopped him on his way to the conference room. By the time he walked in, Sierra was sitting next to Barnes, talking to him. She was smiling unreservedly, as if she was delighted to renew his acquaintance. Sierra had never smiled at Nick that way.

As he got closer, he realized Barnes was telling her about a family vacation. Nick didn't even know the guy was married, let alone had kids.

"Let's get started," he said after shaking Barnes's hand.

An hour later, as the elevator door closed on Walker Barnes, Nick said, "It sounded as if you and Barnes connected. That you really understood what he wanted."

Sierra shrugged. "Some clients are like that, aren't they? You see their vision immediately. Walker was easy to talk to. I'll write up my notes for you."

"No, don't." He shook his head, trying to shed his annoyance. She and Barnes had been so easy together. So natural. As if they'd been friends for years. "It's your project."

"Really?" Her eyes brightened for a moment, then she frowned. "Walker Barnes knows a lot of the big guns in Chicago. I thought you'd want to design the house yourself."

"It'll still be a Boone and Associates house. It's time you tackled a high-profile project."

"Thank you, Nick." She glanced down at the notes she'd taken. "I'll talk to Walker and find out when he wants me to take a look at the site. I'll start working on the preliminary sketches after I've seen it."

"He said his property was on the lake. Is he building on the North Shore?" Nick's mind had wandered as he'd listened to Sierra and Barnes talk. He'd watched her fingers on the pencil as she took notes, studied her body language as she leaned toward their client.

"No." She clutched the legal pad to her chest like a shield, and he remembered her parents had lived on the North Shore. She focused on her pad again, but he didn't think she was reading her notes. "He's building in a small town in Door County, a place called Otter Tail."

"A summer home?"

"No. He lives up there now. He flies to Chicago when he has to." She smiled. "He wants to hear the lake when he wakes up in the morning."

She'd gotten all that from the few minutes she'd talked to him before Nick arrived? "You're going to have to travel up there as the house is being built, you know. Is that all right? You'll probably need several visits besides this preliminary one."

"Of course." She smiled a little too brightly. "I'll do whatever it takes."

As she walked back to her office, Nick watched her go. Maybe they needed to talk about that night, after all, so he could put it out of his mind and move on.

"OH MY GOD, SIERRA." Callie grasped her hands. "Are you sure?"

"I peed on a stick three times. All of them were positive." She squeezed her friend's hands across the white tablecloth of their usual restaurant, begging for a last scrap of hope. "You're a doctor. Those things can be wrong, can't they?"

"If you take the test too early, they can. But you'd be two and a half months along. If three tests came up positive, you're pregnant."

Sierra slumped in her chair. Callie's words were so final. So definite. But deep down, Sierra had known.

It wasn't just the positive tests. The nausea that plagued her, the weariness, her swollen, tender breasts had all prepared her for that pink line. But once Callie said "You're pregnant," once Sierra allowed herself to think *I'm pregnant,* she couldn't pretend it would go away.

"What are you going to do?"

She looked down at her untouched chef's salad, battling the urge to weep. "I have no idea." This, on top of losing her parents, was too much. "I can't think."

"If you need to make an appointment at a…clinic, I'll go with you."

Sierra shook her head. "I can't do that." Another loss would completely destroy her. "I want this baby."

"Okay, then we'll figure it out together." Callie, brisk and efficient, sat up straighter.

"I'm a little worried, Cal." She tried to smile at her friend, but her mouth quivered. "My mom had all those miscarriages. Maybe…maybe I will, too."

"You're going to have to tell Nick."

"I know, but I'll wait a few more weeks." Her throat swelled. "No sense telling him if—if…"

"Yeah, I get it." Callie studied her over the rim of her wineglass. "You want to stay with me for a few days?"

So you're not alone?

Her friend didn't have to say it. Did Sierra look that pathetic? "Thanks, Cal, but I'll be okay."

SIERRA ROLLED HER CHAIR away from her desk and took a deep breath. She would do it tonight. The office had emptied, but Nick was still here.

It had been two weeks since her dinner with Callie, and Sierra had put it off too long. Tonight she would tell Nick she was pregnant. He'd be shocked. Probably upset. But a man had a right to know he was going to be a father.

And if it didn't go well, she would move up her trip to Wisconsin to take a look at Walker Barnes's property.

Nick's office door was open, the light spilling into the hallway. She paused before she reached it, straightening her skirt, her jacket, running a hand over her hair. Then, taking a deep breath, she stepped to the door.

He was looking at her, as if he'd heard her approach. She swallowed once and moved inside. "Nick, we need to talk."

CHAPTER THREE

NICK PUSHED AWAY FROM his desk. "Sierra. Come on in." He straightened his red tie and pushed his rolled-up shirtsleeves a little higher on his arms. She remembered how his arms felt, wrapped around her. Strong. Comforting. Protecting her from the darkness.

His forearms were dusted with dark hair, and she remembered the glide of those hairs across her body, as well.

She took her time easing the door closed as she tried to regain her composure. It was one thing to plan her speech in the quiet of her office. It was quite another to have to look Nick in the eye and tell him she was pregnant with his child.

When she was sure the door had clicked shut, she drew a deep breath and turned around. Nick was still on his feet, watching her calmly. Politely, as if she was merely an employee with a question.

She'd bet he wasn't going to look so polite, or so calm, after she told him her news.

She perched on the edge of the sleek leather couch against the wall, instead of the chair in front of his desk, where she usually sat. Tonight, she needed a little distance. She expected that he would, too.

Nick sank back into his chair, watching her. Waiting. Her heart pounding, her mouth suddenly dry, she tugged her skirt a fraction of an inch lower. This was harder than she'd thought it would be. "We've both been avoiding the subject, but we need to talk about…about what happened in Los Angeles."

Instead of the tension she'd expected those words to cause, his shoulders relaxed. "You're right. We should have cleared the air about this a long time ago. I don't want it to affect our working relationship."

What they wanted didn't matter anymore. A lot more than their working relationship was about to change. "The thing is, Nick, I'm…I'm…"

When she couldn't get the word out, he jumped in. "You're feeling awkward." He smiled. "I am, too." He stood and moved toward her, his long, rangy body filling all the available space in the room. Her heart lurched, then began pounding as he sat next to her on the suddenly too small couch.

He leaned closer, and the scent of his aftershave drifted over her, reminding her vividly of that night. "Neither one of us should feel that way. You'd just had a horrible shock. You were upset, you weren't thinking straight, and you needed company. I was just helping you out." He took her hand and held it between his. They were warm and smooth. Strong. When she thought about his hands on her, how she'd begged him to touch her, she eased away.

"Yes, it's been awkward since that night," she said, studying his blue eyes for a hint of what he was feeling. Nothing. He would be a good poker player. "That's not what this is about."

His body shifted back, away from her. Was it conscious? She didn't think so. "What then? Regret? Not necessary. You needed comfort. I was glad I could give that to you."

Yes, she'd needed to feel something other than grief and pain, and he'd given her that. She'd asked him to. She was still struggling with why she had. "I…I wasn't myself that night."

The fabric of his slacks whispered across the leather of the couch as he slid farther away. "Of course you weren't. How could you be? People do…they do uncharacteristic things when they're under stress. Let's just chalk it up to that and move on."

If only it was that easy. "It's a little late for that, Nick."

"What, then?" His eyebrows pulled together in confusion. "What do you want, Sierra? Do you want me to say I'm sorry?"

He stood abruptly and picked up the rake from the tiny zen garden that sat on the cabinet. He concentrated fiercely on drawing even lines through the sand. "I'll apologize if it will make you feel better, but you're blowing this all out of proportion. The sex was…it was relaxation. You needed a distraction. It was nothing."

It was nothing. Was that how he felt about making love? That it was casual recreation? That it had no meaning? She slowly relaxed her clenched hands and met his gaze again. "I needed someone to stay with me. To hold me so I wasn't alone. Making love was a mistake, but I wouldn't have done it if I didn't have some feelings for you."

He blanched at the word *feelings,* and she was proud of herself for not flinching. For staying calm. Cool. "Of course I have feelings for you. We work together. I see you every day. I have feelings for Janet, and for Bob in the office next to mine, and for Phil the janitor. I didn't say I was madly in love with you." She closed her eyes and took a deep breath to steady herself. Maybe her hormones were making her a little emotional. She stood up and paced the room.

She *had* asked him to have sex with her, and they hadn't been in a relationship. That could be interpreted as taking sex as lightly as he did. "In spite of the way it seemed that night, I don't…I don't usually do that. I don't jump into bed with a guy on a whim. So if I gave you the wrong message, I'm sorry. That night was completely out of character for me."

Before she told him about the baby, she needed to make sure he understood. She didn't want him to think that someone else could be the father. She needed to make it clear that there was no question the baby was his.

He walked back over to her, and she held her ground. When he took her hand, she resisted the impulse to snatch it away. "It doesn't matter, Sierra. We're both adults. We're allowed to have sex if we want to. It was just sex. A moment in time. We've both moved on."

His words were an arrow to her heart, quick and painful. She snatched her hand away. "Actually, Nick, it turns out we haven't moved on. I'm pregnant."

"What?" The color drained from his face. "That's not possible. We used a condom."

"Condoms can fail."

Devastation stared at her out of his eyes. "Goddamn it all to hell. Tell me this is your idea of a joke."

Another stab to her heart, this one a little sharper. "My God, Nick! I wouldn't joke about this. I'm going to have a baby. You're going to be a father."

"Don't use that word," he said sharply. "I can't be a father."

"In about six months, you will be."

"No, I won't." He dropped onto the edge of his desk. "I can't do this, Sierra. Won't do it. This is the last thing I ever wanted."

"You don't have a choice, Nick." It was hard to speak over the ache in her chest. "It's reality."

He stared at her, his eyes dark with panic. Denial. "I don't want children. I don't even want to think about children. A kid would ruin my life."

Echoes of the unbearable pain from the night her parents had died slid through her. She pressed her palm to her abdomen, felt the slight swelling of her womb. Cupped it, as if she could prevent the baby from hearing what its father was saying. "Ruin your life? That's pretty extreme."

"It's how I feel."

Her hand dropped as she studied Nick's lean, angular face, his bright blue eyes, his thick, dark hair. She'd always thought he was attractive. Before the night in Los Angeles, she'd had a little crush on him.

Looking at him now, her crush vanished into a distant memory. Nick's handsome face was just the glittery wrapping on an empty package.

"I can't be part of this, but I can give you money. You'll have expenses. Doctor's appointments. The kind of things pregnant women have to do." He opened his checkbook, scribbled something, tore off the check and walked around the desk. He stood at a careful distance from her, as if he was in danger of catching a disease. "If you need more, let me know." The check fluttered in front of her, as if his hand was shaking.

What had she ever found attractive about him? He took a careful step closer, holding out the piece of paper that represented what her baby was worth to its father. Nick thought handing her money absolved him of all responsibility. That she would walk away and he could forget all about this conversation.

Did he think she would put his response out of her mind? That she would be able to continue working for him?

Her stomach lurched and she struggled to draw in a breath. "You'll understand why I'm submitting my resignation, effective immediately. I'll have a letter on your desk in the morning."

"That's not necessary. Your employment here has

nothing to do with…" He glanced at her abdomen, then looked quickly away.

She refused to let him see how devastating his words were. As she backed toward the door, she fumbled for the doorknob. Just when she found it, she felt it twist. She stumbled to the side as someone pushed the door open.

A tall, slender woman peeked around the edge. Her hair hung past her shoulders in dark waves, and she wore a severely tailored business suit that couldn't hide her curves. Even with minimal makeup, she was stunning.

Her eyes hardened when she saw Sierra. "Nicky. Am I interrupting?"

His cheeks reddened. "Go wait in the conference room, Jasmine. I'm busy."

As the woman's footsteps retreated down the hall, Sierra wondered how she knew where the room was. Images of Nick and the woman, the huge conference room table, filled her head. Her stomach suddenly queasy, Sierra reached for the door again. "You're busy, and I don't want to keep you."

"Take this, then." He shoved the check in her direction. "It's my responsibility."

Fighting nausea, she pulled the door open and fled. She barely made it to the washroom before she threw up.

NICK HEARD THE BATHROOM door shut behind Sierra, and wanted to follow her inside. Beg her to say she was joking.

Pregnant. He paced the office as he thought about what it meant. Sierra was going to have a baby. His baby. A human being he would be tethered to forever.

A child he might get attached to.

A child who could get hurt or sick. Or worse.

Someone who could leave him, just as his mother had done.

He stared, unseeing, at the skyline of Chicago. Dusk bruised the sky, and dark clouds obscured the moon. He heard the bathroom door open again, and he reached for the bottle of scotch he kept in the small wooden cabinet next to the couch.

He couldn't be a father. The bottle clinked against the rim of the glass as he poured, and the smooth single malt burned all the way to his stomach. He didn't know the first thing about being a parent. Didn't want to learn.

He didn't want any attachments. Any strings. His life was perfect the way it was.

He swallowed the rest of the scotch in the glass.

Sierra had turned so pale when he offered her the money. She'd looked the way she had that night. Shocked. Devastated. As if she were falling into a dark, bottomless pit. He'd wanted to help her. Calm her. The sex had been nothing more than that.

She'd called it making love.

He didn't do that, either.

Hands shaking, he reached for the bottle again and poured another two fingers. The carefully built structure of his life was crumbling around him. Crashing in on itself, disappearing as he watched.

He lifted the glass of scotch, stared at the amber liquid, then set it back down. He didn't need the drink. He was in control.

His fingers bumped the perpetual motion toy on his desk, and the five silver balls suspended by strings began to move. They clacked against each other, each sharp sound punctuating his dread.

There was no room for a child in his life. Children were vulnerable. Helpless. Completely dependent on their parents' whims. They came with a lifetime of strings.

Strings too easily broken.

Attachments that led only to pain. Loss. Rejection.

He was in control of his own life now, and he kept it free of strings.

He'd never worried about getting a woman pregnant. He always used a condom, even if his partner was using birth control. He batted at the metal balls of the toy, and they moved faster. The noise bounced off the walls, magnified, mocked him. Control could be snatched away from him in one careless moment.

He grabbed the strings and stopped the balls from moving, and the room went silent.

Why hadn't he gotten a vasectomy?

This…this problem would turn out all right. Sierra couldn't want to be a mother. She'd just suffered a crushing loss. She was struggling to deal with her parents' estate.

He stared down at the check he'd dropped onto his desk. She hadn't taken it.

He'd go talk to her. Make her see reason. Convince her to make the right decision. His hand shook as he set the glass carefully on the cabinet. He hadn't heard the elevator, so she must still be here.

He headed for his office door, but as he opened it, Jasmine appeared, frowning.

"What's going on, Nick? I thought we had a date."

"We did, but something came up." He took her arm and steered her toward the elevator. When he glanced down the hall, he saw Sierra's dark red head bent over her desk. He grabbed his wallet from his pocket and pulled out a handful of bills. "Take a cab home, and we'll have dinner another time. All right?"

Why had he thought Jasmine's eyes were so intriguing? Right now, they just looked calculating. "I had plans for this evening. I left a lot of work on my desk to spend it with you," she said with a pout.

"Sorry, honey. I have some business to take care of."

The elevator dinged, the door opened, but she didn't budge. She glanced toward Sierra. "I'll wait."

Nick followed her gaze, then dragged Jasmine into the elevator. "I'm flattered, Jazz, but it's not going to happen. Not tonight."

All the way to the ground floor, she leaned against the wall in the corner of the elevator, her arms crossed over her chest. He could see the wheels spinning in her head as she watched his reflection in the shiny metal door. When the elevator opened, he practically dragged her out of the building. By the time he managed to hail a cab and say good-night, dusk had deepened to darkness.

The elevator seemed to move with excruciating slowness. He watched the indicator count off the floors until it reached his. As soon as the doors opened, he hurried to Sierra's office.

She was gone.

Her computer was centered on her desk and her briefcase and coat were missing. His chest tightened until he caught sight of her pictures and books on her bookcase. She wasn't gone for good. She'd be in tomorrow, and he could talk to her then.

He stood in the middle of her small office, gazing at the sketches of houses she'd designed that hung on the walls, along with her diploma from the University of Illinois and several photographs of a stand of maple trees, the sun reflecting off their bright green leaves. A clump of birch trees stood off to the side.

She'd said she'd have her resignation on his desk tomorrow. He'd get here early and wait for her, and they'd talk again. This time, he'd be the one in control.

CHAPTER FOUR

SIERRA STOOD AT THE WINDOW, looking down on the city she loved. The moon hung over Lake Michigan, its glowing yellow light reflecting off the dark water, illuminating Chicago's beautiful skyline. She'd always enjoyed her office, with its panoramic view of the lake and high-rises. Tonight, the sight of the city laid out before her brought a lump to her throat.

That was good, she told herself. She should feel something when she left the job she'd held for the past three years. Since the scene with Nick earlier that evening, she'd felt as if she'd been dipped in novocaine.

She hadn't thought about what she'd do tomorrow. She'd been focused on getting away, on putting as much distance between herself and Nick as possible. The picture of him standing in front of her, holding out a check, was burned into her brain.

She'd fled from the images and retreated to her condo on the North Side. Then she'd gathered empty boxes and forced herself to drive back downtown. She had to do this tonight. To make a clean break.

As she sorted through her drawers, she dropped her own belongings into a box and made a neat pile of office supplies on top of her desk. She focused carefully on the job to make sure she didn't take anything that had come from the supply closet.

The last drawer held her files—plans for the buildings she'd worked on, the projects she had pending. As she thumbed through them, the names brought back memories. Working with Nick on an office building. Designing one on her own, with him looking over her shoulder. The first house she'd designed by herself.

They belonged to the company, but she would take copies of some of them. She'd need them in her portfolio when she looked for another job. She picked out five projects that showed different designs, different uses of space, and set them on her desk to copy. As she was closing the drawer, she saw the Barnes file.

The manila file folder was new and still uncreased. She'd finished the preliminary drawings and had planned to drive to Otter Tail sometime in the next week and show them to Jen and Walker Barnes.

The folder slid easily through her fingers as she studied it. Wondered. Had a flicker of an idea.

There was nothing left for her in Chicago. Her job had helped her get through the days since her parents' death, but now that was gone, too. All that was left were raw memories.

Maybe later, being in the city wouldn't be so painful. Right now, walking into her condo reminded her of the day her parents had helped her move in. Riding the El past Wrigley Field reminded her of all the games she'd attended there with her mom and dad. Running along the lakefront path reminded her of the days she'd spent sailing with them in the summer.

She'd cleaned out her parents' house and put it up for sale. She'd spent weekends sorting through everything, storing what she wanted to keep and donating or selling the rest. She'd found her mom's journals, but hadn't been able to read them yet.

Sierra turned away from the beautiful skyline. She loved Chicago. She'd come back eventually. But right now, everything she saw or did reminded her of her parents. Coming into the Loop every day, to work at another architectural firm, would be a daily reminder of Nick. Of the fact that he didn't want his child.

She needed a change.

Ignoring the flicker of guilt, she set the Barnes file in the pile to be copied.

As NICK GOT OFF THE ELEVATOR that morning, his gaze went immediately to Sierra's office. She wasn't there.

That meant she hadn't delivered her resignation letter yet.

He ignored the uneasiness that stirred. He'd gotten into the habit of looking for her when he arrived every morning, and she was almost always at her desk, her head bent over her work.

Last night had been…difficult. She'd probably over-slept.

With a last glance over his shoulder at her empty office, he stepped into his own. Janet followed him in and closed the door.

"What's up?" he asked. "Did you get those estimates from the alternate contractor for the Willis job?"

As he dropped his briefcase on the couch, a mental picture of Sierra sitting there the night before flashed through his head.

"No. I don't have the Willis estimates." She picked up a piece of paper that had been centered on his desk. "What's this about?"

He took it from her. Two lines on the firm's letterhead stationery confirmed Sierra's resignation. They were followed by her signature, the date.

Nothing more.

She'd gotten to the office before him, after all.

"What does it look like? Sierra resigned." His hand tightened on the sheet of paper, then he dropped it onto his desk.

"You knew this was coming, and you let her go?"

"What was I supposed to do? Chain her to her chair?"

Janet raised one eyebrow. "Was there a problem? I thought you liked her work."

"I did, but we'll hire another associate. We get a couple of applications every week, don't we?"

"Why did she resign, Nick?" His admin assistant looked at the letter, as if hoping it would provide a clue.

"It was personal. She's still recovering from her parents' deaths." *And he'd just caused another wound.* He ignored the guilt. "She needed a change."

Janet held his gaze. "Really? She told me that this

job was helping her cope. Giving her something else to focus on. So what happened?"

"How the hell should I know?" He crumpled the letter and tossed it in the trash. "She resigned. She's gone."

Janet stood backlit in a patch of sunlight that left her face in shadow. But he knew what he'd see if she stepped closer. Disapproval. Disappointment. "Fine," she finally said. "You're the boss."

"Bring me the applications we've saved. I'll work on finding someone to take her place. And I'll need her files to reassign her work."

"I'll get on that right away, boss." Janet headed for the door.

When she started calling him boss, it meant she was seriously pissed off. "What? What's wrong?"

She spun around to face him. "Even you can't be so dense. What did you do?" She waited a beat. "Did something happen between you?"

"Why would you think that? I've been nothing but professional with her in the office. Strictly business." Out of the office was a different story. One that his admin didn't need to hear.

Janet sighed. "Sierra is a beautiful young woman. Generous. Friendly to everyone. She lights up a room when she walks in." She narrowed her eyes. "I've seen you watching her lately, when you thought no one was looking. It's not hard to connect the dots."

"There are no dots."

"Then why are you yelling?"

"I'm not…" He snatched Sierra's letter out of the trash and smoothed out the creases. "Bring me her employment file so I can add this and make a few notes."

"Sure, boss." Janet headed out of the office.

"And cut out the *boss* crap," he called after her. The only answer was the clicking of the door as it shut behind her. Nick sighed as he dropped into his desk chair.

He knew all the architects in Chicago. It shouldn't be hard to find out where Sierra had gone. He'd make sure she took that check. Whatever she decided to do, she would need money. It was all he had to give her.

SIERRA LEANED AGAINST the back of the booth at the Harp and Halo Pub in Otter Tail, sipping the ginger ale the blonde woman had given her. Delaney. She was the drummer in the band playing tonight.

When Sierra told Jen and Walker Barnes that she had something to discuss with them, they'd suggested meeting at this pub. Jen would be working, she'd said, but she could get away for a while to discuss Sierra's design ideas. And as a side benefit, the band was really good.

Sierra had been here a couple days already, although Jen and Walker didn't know that, and this was the first time they could both meet with her. Sierra was so tired of being cooped up in the sterile, too quiet motel room that she'd ignored the nausea churning in her stomach and driven over early.

Only to end up on her knees in front of the toilet in the ladies' room.

She shouldn't have told Delaney she was pregnant. Delaney had told Maddie, the owner of the pub. Maddie could tell someone else. Jen and Walker could find out before Sierra was ready to let them know.

The alternative had been letting Delaney think she was drunk. Jen and Walker would probably have heard that, too.

"Hey, Sierra." Maddie put a baked potato on the table. "Early in my pregnancy, I couldn't eat much, either. But a baked potato always seemed to settle my stomach." She smiled as she patted her huge belly. "It's on the house. Maybe it will help."

The potato had been split open and steam rose from the fluffy white interior. A small dish of butter sat next to it. Surprisingly, Sierra's stomach didn't revolt when she smelled it.

"Thanks, Maddie." She managed a weary smile. "I'll try it."

"Are you visiting someone in town?" Maddie asked.

Sierra poked at the potato with her fork. "I'm hoping to be working for Jen and Walker Barnes. Do you know them?" It wouldn't hurt to gather some information about her prospective employers. She'd met with both of them a couple of times, but she'd been Nick's employee then. Now she needed any advantage she could get.

"Jen is one of my best friends." Maddie slid into the

booth across from Sierra. "You don't mind, do you? My feet are killing me."

"Of course not," she managed to say. "It's nice to have company." Maddie was one of Jen's best friends? Sierra's stomach began to churn again. Maddie would definitely tell Jen she was pregnant.

Before she could ask her to keep the news to herself, the other woman said, "Mind if I ask what you're going to do for Jen and Walker?"

Sierra sighed. She'd already told Maddie she wanted to work for them. She might as well tell her the rest. "I'm an architect. I'm hoping they hire me to design and help build their house."

"Cool. So you'll be here for a while?"

"I hope so."

"I go to a prenatal exercise class in Sturgeon Falls twice a week. If you'd like to come, I'd love company on the drive."

"Thanks. I'll think about it." As soon as Sierra's stomach stopped lurching at the though of exercising.

"No pressure," Maddie said with a smile. "But it's fun to be around other pregnant women. We compare symptoms and curse our husbands for getting us in this condition."

"No husband to curse." Sierra tried to smile.

"Boyfriends, too," Maddie said with a laugh. "They're all fair game."

"No boyfriend." Sierra's hand tightened on the fork as she realized she'd spoken out loud. She stared at the potato, wishing Maddie would disappear.

Instead, the other woman leaned closer. Sierra felt her gaze, but concentrated on stirring the butter into the potato.

"If you'd like to talk, I'm always here," Maddie said after a moment, her voice soft. "I'm a good listener."

"Thanks," Sierra said. "I'll keep that in mind." She stared at the plate, willing her to leave.

After a moment, Maddie nodded and slid out of the booth. As she walked away, Sierra stared after her. That was it? No lecture? No prying questions? Only sympathy?

Sierra's gaze swept over the already crowded pub. People leaned against the bar or stood in small groups next to it. Most of the tables were full of couples and families, and she heard a lot of laughter.

Delaney had helped her when she got sick. Maddie had offered compassion and a ride to a prenatal exercise class. For the first time since she arrived in Otter Tail, Sierra took a deep breath and let some of her tension go. Maybe this would work out. She was good at what she did, and she already knew Jen and Walker liked her design. She could convince them to hire her. Two people had reached out to her. Maybe this small town in northern Wisconsin would turn out to be a good place to stay.

The murmur of voices, the clinking of glasses, washed over her. Instead of annoying her, it was comforting. Sierra took a bite of the potato. Her stomach didn't rebel, so she took another bite. Then another.

Fifteen minutes later, she'd finished almost the whole

thing. Maddie was right; it had helped. As Sierra sipped on her ginger ale and watched the band prepare to play, someone slid into the booth across from her.

Jen. And Walker.

Jen wore white pants and a white shirt with The Summer House embroidered on the pocket. Sierra had already found out Jen was owner and chef of the restaurant on Main Street. She settled in the booth with a smile.

"Hey, Sierra," she said, glancing at the remnants of potato skin. "Is that all you had for dinner?"

"I wasn't very hungry," Sierra answered.

Walker smiled as he linked his fingers with his wife. "Jen is a chef. Her mission in life is to feed people."

"I've heard wonderful things about your restaurant," Sierra said. "I can't wait to try it."

Walker released his wife's hand and studied Sierra. "Is there a problem with the house?"

"Not at all." She took a deep breath and folded her arms on the table. "I've resigned from Boone and Associates, but I took a copy of your house design with me. I put together a proposal for you to consider." She picked up the packet lying on the seat next to her and edged it toward the couple. "I would love to work directly with you to finish the design and supervise the construction."

Walker glanced at the report cover, but didn't touch it. "You've left Nick?"

"I didn't leave Nick. I left Boone and Associates," she said, a little too sharply. She swallowed. "You seemed to like what I've done so far, and I could devote all my time to your project."

"Why didn't you just call us?" Jen asked.

"I felt our conversation would be better in person than on the phone." It was harder to say no that way. "I wanted to show you what I've done since last time we talked."

Walker's gaze sharpened. "Always smart to do business face-to-face," he murmured with a nod. He opened the folder and glanced at her drawing of the exterior of the house, then flipped the pages to the renderings of each room. "You've done a lot of work on this."

"I want this job."

Walker closed the folder. "Do you mind if I ask why you quit?"

She'd expected him to ask. "That's a fair question." She pressed her fingers into the table, watching the tips turn red. It was harder to answer than she'd expected it to be. She didn't want to sound weak. Or emotional. Even though she'd never been more emotional in her life. "My parents died three months ago. They were killed in a plane crash." She swallowed. "I've had...it's been very hard. Selling their house, going through all their things..."

She blinked and stared out the front window. Darkness had descended since she arrived, and she couldn't see beyond the pub. "I needed to get away from Chicago, at least for a while. There were too many memories there.

"I thought working on your house was the perfect solution."

"You couldn't do that and still work for Nick?"

"Nick wouldn't be able to let me stay up here for the entire construction. I'd be working on other projects at the same time." She shrugged, hoping it looked offhand. "Nick focuses on commercial work, and I've found I prefer to concentrate on residential projects. It seemed like a good time to part ways."

"And you took a client with you," Walker said, watching her.

"Yes, I did."

"Does Boone know?"

"Does it matter?"

"I'll take that as a no. He's not going to be happy."

A rush of irritation flooded her nerves. "With all due respect, Walker, designing your house isn't quite the same as designing a skyscraper in downtown Chicago. Nick will be annoyed, because he's a competitive guy. But the amount of money he would have made on your house is minuscule compared to his other projects. I don't think he's going to lose a lot of sleep over it."

Jen's lips twitched and she leaned against her husband. "I guess she told you, big shot."

Walker's serious expression eased as he wrapped his arm around her. "I guess she did."

"Not many people stand up to Walker," Jen confided. "A little attitude is good for him."

Sierra felt her face redden. "I didn't mean you're not important. Of course you are. You're a big deal in

Chicago, and I'm sure Nick wants your house in his portfolio. All I meant was that he's not going to go broke because he lost this job. He won't flip out." She hoped he didn't, anyway. And if he did, it would be her he'd resent. Not Walker and Jen.

"We'll take a look at your proposal," Walker said. "I assume you've included your fees and cost projections?"

"Of course. They're very fair. You'll be paying less than you would have paid Boone and Associates."

"But more than you'd be getting from Nick."

"Yes. You'd be getting a full-time supervisor on site. That's more than you would have gotten from B and A."

Walker tapped his fingers on the proposal. "We'll take a look at it and let you know in a day or two."

"Thank you," Sierra said. The churning in her stomach steadied. They hadn't said no. And when they had a chance to study her proposal, they would say yes.

Maddie stopped next to the booth. "Hey, guys, how's it going?"

"Good," Jen said. "How are you?"

"Hanging in there. Counting the days," Maddie answered with a smile. She took the plate with the potato skin off the table. "And happy that I'm not still eating only potatoes." She glanced at Sierra. "Did it help?"

"It did. Thank you," she managed to say.

Jen and Walker went perfectly still as they stared at her. Walker's mouth was a hard line.

"You're pregnant," he said, his voice flat. It wasn't a question.

"That's not relevant."

His eyebrows snapped together. "You're going to be spending time at a construction site. Crawling up ladders, working around dangerous equipment, doing physical work. Of course it's relevant."

Sierra gripped the edge of the bench seat. "I'm fit and healthy and perfectly capable of doing this job. My pregnancy isn't a factor."

"It's a liability issue for both me and the contractor," he retorted, drumming his fingers on the tabletop.

"Believe me, I'll be careful. I'm not going to take any risks. Why would I take chances with my baby?"

"You're a lawsuit waiting to happen."

Every sound in the pub was suddenly magnified. Voices were shriller. Silverware rattled and crashed together. Clinking glasses were unbearably high-pitched.

Sierra pressed her hand to her abdomen. The potato hadn't been a good idea, after all. Walker wasn't going to hire her. Her fingernails cut into her palm and her chest tightened. All her plans had revolved around working for Walker and Jen. Of having a job far away from Chicago.

Who else would hire her, once they found out she was pregnant?

"I'll have an attorney write up a document that completely absolves you of liability," she said, her mouth almost too dry to speak. "I want to help build your house, Walker."

He shook his head. "I love your ideas. I love the preliminary designs. But I just don't see how this can work. It's too dangerous." He pushed the project report across the table. Back to her.

Jen put her hand on his arm. "Hold on a second," she murmured to her husband. "Maybe you should tell us more about your personal situation, Sierra. Is your baby's father with you?"

Her words were like a slap in the face. "That's not your concern. It's irrelevant." Sierra glanced at Walker. "And you've clearly made up your mind already."

"You're here in Otter Tail by yourself." Again, it was not a question. Walker's voice was even. No inflection. Impossible to read. No wonder he was such a successful businessman.

Just like Nick.

"Yes."

"I can't hire you, Sierra." Walker's voice softened. "I'm sorry, but I can't have a pregnant woman on a construction site. Maybe I can find some other job for you that won't involve the house."

"No, thank you. I'm an architect. I don't want some make-work job." She hated the pity in his voice. "If I can't work on your project, I'll find another one." She fumbled in her purse for the money to pay for her ginger ale and potato. Her fingers shook as she tried to remove some bills from her wallet.

Finally she pulled out a ten and dropped it on the

table. "I'll make sure you get the rest of the material I've put together for your house," she said as she stood up. She hurried toward the door, tears blurring her vision. Delaney swiveled on the stool behind her drums and watched her leave.

Sierra was unlocking her Honda Civic when someone touched her arm. "You forgot your coat," Jen said.

Sierra yanked the door open, tossed the spring jacket on the passenger seat, then slid in. "Thanks." She tried to pull the door closed, but it wouldn't budge.

Jen was holding it open. "I'm pregnant, too," she said quietly. "We just found out. No one else knows, and Walker is…he's acting like an idiot."

"Congratulations." Sierra started the engine. "Let go of the door, please." She had to leave before she broke down in front of Jen. That would complete her humiliation. She tugged on the handle, but Jen tugged back.

"Listen to me. He's completely overreacting to this. He wants me to stop working at the restaurant. He expects me to sit at home for the next eight months and twiddle my thumbs."

"What your husband wants for you has nothing to do with me." Sierra pulled on the door again, and Jen jerked it out of her hand.

"Yes, it does. There are reasons why he's being so overprotective, reasons that have nothing to do with you. But you're getting the blowback. I'll straighten him out." Her voice softened. "We'll figure out a way to hire you."

A tear dripped onto the steering wheel, and Sierra

wiped it away. She'd cried more in the last few months than she had during the rest of her life, and she was sick of it. "I'll find another job."

"I don't want you to find another job," Jen said softly. "I want you to stay in Otter Tail and build our house."

"Yeah, well, your husband doesn't. I'm not going to get in the middle of that." Sierra wrenched the door shut, and when Jen reached out her hand, she stared at it until the woman stepped back. Then Sierra accelerated out of the parking lot.

It was too late to check out of the motel tonight. Her weariness went all the way to her bones. She'd sleep tonight, and tomorrow she'd leave.

But she had no idea where she would go.

CHAPTER FIVE

SIERRA HADN'T UNPACKED more than one small suit-case, so it didn't take long to get ready to leave the next morning. As she walked from her room to the motel office, the sky was bright blue and the air smelled fresh. Full of promise. The trees were getting ready to bud out, and everything was waiting, poised on the brink of new life.

Myrtle Sanders, the owner of the Bide-a-Wee Motel, looked up when she walked in the door. "Hi, Ms. Clark," the woman said in a raspy voice. "What can I do for you?"

"I'm checking out," Sierra answered.

Myrtle's eyebrows rose. "I thought you were going to be here for a while. What happened?"

"Things changed," Sierra said. She put her credit card on the counter. "Your motel was very nice."

The older woman swiped it through the machine. "Saw you at the Harp last night. Did you enjoy the music?"

"I didn't stay long enough to hear them."

"Too bad." Myrtle put the credit card on the counter, along with the receipt to sign. "If you're staying in the area, make sure you come back to hear them next Friday."

"I will. Thanks, Ms. Sanders." Sierra's face felt as if it would crack when she smiled. She scribbled her signature, then tried to take her credit card back. Myrtle had her hand on it, holding it in place.

"Call me Myrtle," she said, studying her. "So where are you headed?"

"I'm not sure." Sierra tugged at the credit card, and she let it go.

"You in trouble, hon?" she asked softly.

Sierra jerked her head up to meet Myrtle's eyes. Did she know? Had the gossip spread already? "I'm…I'm fine," she finally said. "But thanks for asking."

"I could reduce the rate on the room." Myrtle watched her shrewdly. "Not much business yet. I'd like to keep the place full."

"I don't know where I'm going," Sierra answered.

"Have something to eat at the Cherry Tree before you make up your mind," Myrtle said. "They do a nice breakfast."

Myrtle needed her money, and where else was Sierra going to go? "I'll think about it," she said.

"Hope to see you again, hon," the motel owner said as Sierra opened the door.

"Thanks."

THE CHERRY TREE WAS ALMOST full, but she got a booth along the wall. She opened the Green Bay newspaper she'd bought from the box outside the diner, but when she found herself starting the same article three times, she closed it again.

After ordering oatmeal and fruit, she opened to the classifieds. There were jobs for administrative assistants, for accountants, for bookkeepers. Jobs for salesmen.

Nothing for architects. She pushed the paper away when her oatmeal arrived. She'd go online. It had been foolish to look at a newspaper, anyway. Architectural firms didn't advertise openings in newspapers. They did it in professional journals and newsletters. Online specialty job sites. Word of mouth.

She let the spoon drop onto the plate beneath her bowl. Word of mouth wasn't going to get her a job. She'd walked out on Nick and taken his client.

She stared out the window blindly as she sipped her herbal tea. She put her hand over her abdomen, imagined she could feel life beneath it. *We'll be fine. I'll find a job. Even if I don't, we have enough money to last for a little while.*

"Mind if I join you?"

She looked up to see Jen standing next to her table. "Help yourself."

"Hey, Jen," the waitress said as she hurried over with a pot of coffee. "We were at your place the other night. Great food."

Jen put her hand over her mug. "Thanks, Sandy. No coffee today. How about some herbal tea?"

Sandy frowned. "Sure, if that's what you want. You off coffee?"

"Stomach's a little upset," Jen answered. "I thought herbal would be better."

"No problem."

When the waitress left, Jen said, "Myrtle told me you were heading out of town."

Sierra pushed her bowl away, and the spoon clattered to the table. "My God! Is there some kind of network that keeps track of everyone in this town? Do you twitter people's locations every fifteen minutes?"

Jen laughed. "No, but thanks for the suggestion. Some people would be all over that idea." Her smile disappeared. "I stopped by the motel to see you, and Myrtle told me you'd already checked out. I'm glad you decided to stop for breakfast."

Sierra raised one shoulder. "It's better if you eat, even if you don't feel like it. In case you've been sick."

Jen leaned across the table and her blond ponytail swung over her shoulder. "The walls have ears in this place," she said quietly. "They all know me. I used to work here. Okay?"

"I understand." No pregnancy talk. "I assume you're here because of the house. I was going to stop by on my way out of town with the file. I have it right here."

She dug through her large bag, pulled out the manila folder and set it on the table. "Good luck with it. Nick has the original, but he doesn't have the work I've done since I left. He'd probably like the project back, and he'll do a good job for you. He's a very talented architect. If you really like my design, he'll use it. He won't have a hissy fit and insist on a new one."

"Nick Boone, the king of control, throws hissy fits? I'd pay to see that."

Sierra had seen him out of control only once. "I was speaking theoretically. I've hardly even heard him raise his voice."

"Well, it won't happen this time, either. Walker and I talked last night. He's not completely convinced, but we want to give you a chance. He's going to insist on a couple of things, but we want to try to make it work. We both love the design, and it wouldn't feel right to take your work and pay someone else to build the house."

"So you'll hire me, but with lots of reservations." She sat straighter on the uncomfortable vinyl bench. She wanted to say no, to stand up and walk away. But desperation couldn't afford pride.

Jen shrugged. "It's the best we can do. Walker may be overreacting, but his concerns are legitimate. Construction sites *are* dangerous. Pregnant women *are* off balance and occasionally clumsy. We'd feel horrible if you got hurt, and frankly, I don't want that on my conscience. Even with a letter from your lawyer, absolving us of any responsibility."

Sierra lifted a large spoonful of oatmeal and watched as heavy clumps dropped into the bowl. "So you're offering me a pity job."

"It's not a pity job. If you weren't pregnant, we'd hire you without a second thought. But being pregnant changes everything."

Yes. It did. She tightened her grip on the spoon, then

set it carefully on the plate. "What 'things' does Walker want?"

Jen relaxed against the back of the booth. "Hard hat at all times. No ladders. You can't be at the site alone. When you're on the site, one of the contractors has to be there, too."

Sierra's face burned, and she clenched her mug of tea tightly. "I'm not a child, Jen. I don't need a babysitter. I've been on construction sites, and I know how to be careful."

"Of course you do." She glanced at the remains of Sierra's oatmeal, and as the waitress appeared with her tea, she said, "I'll have some of that, please, Sandy."

Jen leaned closer to Sierra. "Walker is worried about me, and I laugh at him. As I said last night, you're getting the blowback. But those are the rules he's insisting on. If you want the job, you're going to have to suck it up."

Humiliation scalded her, and Sierra pressed her lips together. "Any other 'things' I should know about before I take the job? Do I have to schedule regular naps? Will he need to make sure I'm taking my vitamins?"

Jen grinned. "I like you. Please take the job. I'll try to keep Walker off your back, but right now, he's in his 'protect the women and children' mode. He'll probably hover for a while, but I'm guessing you can deal with that." She studied Sierra for a moment, her eyes shrewd. "I'm guessing you can deal with just about anything."

The smell of bacon frying and toast burning made

her stomach roll. Sierra ate a spoonful of cold oatmeal. "You do what you have to do."

"So you'll take the job?"

"I'll think about it." Last night, she'd come too close to begging, and she burned with shame at the memory. Today, she wasn't going to jump at the offer. Desperation made you vulnerable.

The waitress slid a bowl of oatmeal in front of Jen and walked away. Jen waited until she was out of earshot before saying, "God, you're tough. How long do you hold a grudge?"

"Grudges are a luxury I can't afford." Sierra laid a hand over her abdomen. "I have to think of what's best for me and the…for me. I don't want to have to second-guess myself constantly. I don't want to look over my shoulder all the time."

"Fair enough." Jen stirred her oatmeal, and the scent drifted across the table. Sierra took another spoonful from her own half-finished bowl. Even cold, it settled her stomach.

"There's an apartment above my restaurant," Jen said. "Let me finish this, then we can take a look at it. Walker and I thought you might like to stay there while you're here. We'll give you a good deal, and it will feel more like home than the motel."

Even after being so reluctant to hire her, Jen and Walker were offering her a place to stay? "I'll take a look at it," she said cautiously.

"It's a little outdated," Jen warned. "But it's conve-nient." She drank some of her tea and grimaced. "It's going to be tough to get used to this. So tell me about Chicago. Have you lived there your whole life?"

NICK TOOK ONE LAST LOOK at the CAD screen on his computer, clicked Save and closed it. The client would be pleased. He'd taken the software company's vision for their headquarters and turned it into a statement of purpose as well as a functional work space. An elegant melding of vision and practicality.

Exactly what they'd said they wanted. His presentation was in a week, and he'd be ready.

He shut down his computer, shoved some folders into his briefcase and grabbed his suit jacket. He didn't have any plans other than a quiet evening at home, working.

He'd spent quite a few nights by himself in the last couple weeks. The club scene had felt flat and boring lately, and he'd broken things off with Jasmine. A necklace from Tiffany's had been a preemptive strike against the tears and clinging he hated.

As he was heading out of his office, he heard giggling coming from the other side of the door. It wouldn't be his admin—Janet was far too dignified to giggle. One of the other administrative assistants must be talking to her.

But when he walked through the door, he saw his all-business, decorous assistant speaking gibberish to a baby she held on the edge of her desk. As the child laughed, drool fell from its mouth onto the leather arm of Janet's expensive Herman Miller chair.

And Janet was giggling.

"Who stole my admin and left this…this doppelgänger behind?" he asked.

Janet picked the baby up and turned to him, still smiling. "This is my granddaughter, Lily. My daughter dropped her off a few minutes ago. Lily is staying with us tonight while her parents have an evening to themselves."

The baby turned to him, then reached toward him with both hands. He took a quick step backward.

Janet's smile faded. "They're not contagious," she said. She handed Lily a toy, and the child immediately lost interest in him. "She's at the friendly stage. Everyone is new and interesting."

"I don't know anything about kids."

"Your loss," Janet said mildly. She shifted the baby to her other arm, and the little one laid her downy head on her grandmother's shoulder. "I love to babysit for Lily."

"Your daughter is lucky."

"No, I'm the lucky one." She rubbed the baby's back and the child closed her eyes. "I get an uninterrupted evening of Lily time."

"And your daughter gets time off."

Janet's hand slowed its soothing circles as she studied him. "Time off makes it sound like Ashley is serving a prison sentence. She's getting a break, something all parents need once in a while. She's not a single parent, like I was, but she still needs to spend uninterrupted time with her husband."

"You were a single parent? Frank isn't her father?" Nick had seen them together at the office picnics, and Janet's husband and kid were tight.

"Yes, he's her father, even though Ashley was seven when Frank and I got married. He's her dad, the man who helped me raise her. Just providing sperm doesn't make you a father."

The baby looked as if she had fallen asleep on Janet's shoulder. Complete trust. "Being a single parent must have been tough," Nick said. If she kept the baby, Sierra would be a single parent.

Janet bent to kiss her granddaughter's head, and he couldn't see her eyes. "You have no idea. When I found out I was pregnant, my boyfriend took off like his hair was on fire. I was terrified, and it was tough for a while, but we made it."

Each word she spoke found its mark like a sharp arrow, and Nick tried to see her face. She wasn't talking about him and Sierra. Janet couldn't know Sierra was pregnant and he was the father. "At least your boyfriend paid child support, didn't he?"

She snorted. "Please. I didn't hear from him again until Ashley was a teenager. He gave me some money then, enough to start a college fund, but that was it."

"How does your daughter feel about him?" Nick asked cautiously. Janet never shared personal information with him. They had a business relationship, and that was the way they both preferred it. But suddenly, he wanted to know.

"They talk once in a while, but that's it. He's pretty

much a stranger who shares genes with Ashley. Frank is her father."

Nick stared at the tiny person asleep on Janet's shoulder. What had Sierra said to him? That in six months, he'd be a father.

He wouldn't be, though. He'd be the sperm donor in his child's life.

"Enjoy your evening with her," he said.

Janet smiled as she set the baby in a stroller next to her desk. "Better me than you, right?"

"Yeah." He watched as she gathered her purse and a huge pink quilted bag, slung both over her shoulder and headed for the elevator.

When the door dinged closed behind her, he stood staring at it for a moment. *Ashley's father had taken off like his hair was on fire.*

Just as Nick had. He'd scribbled out a check and tried to buy his way out of his responsibilities.

He reentered his office, dropped his briefcase and pulled Sierra's employment folder out of the drawer. He should have given it back to Janet to store with the files of all the other former employees. He wasn't sure why he hadn't.

The letter she'd written was stark. Formal. No hint of anything personal, no allusion to why she'd really left.

Why would there be? He'd made his feelings very clear.

He wasn't interested. His responsibility ended with money. She was on her own.

He slid his hands into his pockets and stared out the big windows at nighttime in Chicago. A forest of brightly lit skyscrapers pointed toward the heavens, monuments to man's ingenuity and genius.

He studied each of the buildings he'd designed, each of his accomplishments. They were his contribution to the city, the only things he'd ever intended to bring into the world. He could shape those structures, control them, make them exactly what he wanted them to be.

They were his babies. The only kind he wanted.

When he'd designed those buildings, he'd spent months laboring over them. Checking and rechecking their designs and specifications, picking out their flaws, correcting them.

It had been his responsibility as their architect.

Now it was his responsibility to make sure his child had what it needed. And he'd ignored that. Worse, rejected it completely.

That wasn't the kind of man he was. He took his responsibilities seriously. He prided himself on that. On doing the right thing. Always.

The heat of shame scalded his skin, followed by a wave of anger. He didn't want to do this. Didn't want to be a father.

He had no choice.

He grabbed the rake for the Zen garden on the cabinet next to the couch and dragged it through the sand. Some of the sand spilled over the side, and the carefully drawn symmetrical lines disappeared. The meticulously placed stones toppled over. He threw the rake against the wall and stormed out of his office.

CHAPTER SIX

As NICK THUMBED THROUGH his mail the following morning, he saw an envelope from Walker Barnes. He picked up his letter opener, thinking about who he'd assigned to the project. Sierra had been the right choice, and the design she'd started had been beautiful. Bob was an okay choice as her replacement.

Maybe Nick should do it himself. It would be something different for him, a break from multistory office buildings. Barnes had seemed to like Sierra's design, so maybe Nick would start with what she had and flesh it out.

He sliced through the thick envelope and shook out the folded letter. A check slid out of it and landed on his desk, facedown.

He stared at it for a long moment before unfolding the letter. The crackling of the cream-colored stationery seemed to fill the room.

Dear Nick,
    Thanks for all the work you've done on the design for our house. The enclosed check should

cover your expenses so far. Jen and I have decided
to hire someone closer to home to complete the
project.

Barnes had signed it himself.

Nick turned the check over and raised his eyebrows.
It was almost twice Sierra's salary from the past month.
Very generous, considering she hadn't even spent all her
time on the Barnes house.

He fingered the check, studying the signature, the
date, the amount. He'd been fired from projects before,
and he would be again. He prepared for it by getting a
retainer before he started a project. Another when the
design was approved and the contract was signed.

Walker had paid him a retainer, just like the rest of
his clients.

So why was he paying again?

Nick punched the button on his intercom. "Janet,
could you come in here, please?"

Moments later the door opened and his admin walked
in. "Yes?"

He pushed the letter across the desk and watched
as she read it, then picked up the check. She frowned.
"What's this for? His retainer was more than enough
to cover your costs."

"I don't know. Have you talked to him lately?"

"I would have let you know if I had."

Barnes had been enthused about the design. Excited. So what had changed since the last time they'd
spoken?

Sierra wasn't working on the project anymore. As far as he knew, Bob hadn't contacted Barnes yet.

The answer came to Nick in a flash of understanding. He shoved himself away from his desk and reached for the rake for his Zen garden, which he'd thrown against the wall last night, before drawing it carefully through the sand.

"Sierra went up there. She's working for Barnes," he said in a flat voice.

"Why would she do that? It only takes a few months to build a house. Why wouldn't she look for another full-time job?" Janet's voice was cool, as if she suspected the truth. Which was impossible.

"It's the only thing that makes sense. Barnes and his wife loved her design. He told me so, more than once. Then Sierra resigned, and a few weeks later, Barnes pulls his business." Had she told Barnes about the baby? About the way Nick had blown her off?

For the first time, he saw his behavior as another man would see it. No stretch of the imagination would describe it as honorable.

"I have to go up there," he said abruptly. "To talk to Sierra."

"Are you going to try and get her to come back to work?" Janet asked.

"I don't know." He had no idea what he was supposed to do. He knew what he wanted to do—run as far and as fast as he could.

But if he wanted to face himself in the mirror, that wasn't an option.

LIGHT REFLECTING OFF Lake Michigan flashed behind the trees on his right as Nick drove north through Wisconsin. The land was flat, the fields muddy and bare and desolate. Occasionally, he'd pass a sea of black mud pierced by the tips of plowed-under cornstalks. Some of the fields were covered in patchy grass where black-and-white cows grazed. The animals stared at him with dull bovine eyes as he sped past. Why would a city woman like Sierra choose to come up here?

Because it was far away from Chicago. She wouldn't run into him, living up here in cow land.

He touched the pocket of his jacket, where he'd stashed the check. He would apologize. They would talk sensibly. He'd give her the check, and this nightmare would be over.

He'd make an appointment to get a vasectomy as soon as he was back in Chicago.

SIERRA SAT AT THE GLEAMING wooden table in the kitchen of the Barnes' rental house as she waited for Jen and Walker. Walker had let her in, told her to help herself to tea or coffee, then he'd run back upstairs.

Sunlight poured over her shoulder and warmed her back. It bounced off the butter-yellow tiles on the lower half of the wall, wrapping her in sunshine. The delicate red, blue and yellow flowers on the wallpaper above the tiles looked as if they were swaying in the breeze from the open window.

It was a rental house, a temporary place to live, but it

felt like a home. The obvious love Jen and Walker shared was what made it so comfortable. So welcoming.

It was exactly what Sierra wanted for her child. What she would create for herself, even though she'd do it alone.

But as homey, as welcoming as Jen and Walker's house might be, it wasn't an office. Jen's sons from her first marriage were away visiting their father, but Sierra was still in someone's house. She heard footsteps above her. Water running. For a moment, she longed for her peaceful work space at Boone and Associates.

That door was closed for good.

The kettle on the stove began to whistle, and as she stood up to get it, she brushed against the wall. An edge of the wallpaper was curling up, and she pressed it into place. She was like that tiny piece of wallpaper—she needed to be smoothed into place, fastened to something. That's what was wrong—she was in a new town, a new apartment, meeting new people. She needed some glue.

As she poured boiling water over her teabag, she vowed not to feel sorry for herself. She was lucky to be here, working at what she loved. Thankful to have found a refuge for herself and her child when she needed it most.

Fortunate to have the luxury of time to figure out what came next.

As she leaned against the counter and waited for her tea to steep, she forced herself to focus on why she was here. Her hand tightened on the edge of the Formica as she ran over her speech again.

Insurance would cover the cost of replacing the plywood they'd already installed for the first floor of the house. The question was, who had dropped the ball?

She didn't know yet, but she would find out. She'd prove to Jen and Walker that hiring her hadn't been a mistake.

She pushed herself away from the counter and set her tea on the wooden table. She wouldn't be so damn wobbly about this if everything in her life wasn't so unsettled. She was a professional. She knew what she was doing, and she'd solve this problem.

She smoothed her new shirt over her new maternity jeans. She'd resisted wearing them, but she was almost four months pregnant and hadn't been able to button her other jeans. Her shirts had all ridden up her belly. The maternity shirt was jersey and clung to her little bump, and she'd already caught herself staring at it too many times. She actually looked pregnant.

It made the baby seem a lot more real.

It was a constant reminder of her tenuous hold on this job.

Jen and Walker appeared at the kitchen door, and Jen's face was pale. She tried to smile, but her mouth trembled. "Sorry to keep you waiting."

Jen had been sick. Sierra was intimately familiar with how a pregnant woman looked after she'd been kneeling in front of a toilet. "Don't worry about it," she said. She gestured to the kettle. "The water's hot, if you want tea."

Jen sank onto a chair and Walker wordlessly fixed her a cup. "What's up?" he asked.

Sierra's fingers tightened on her own cup, then she set it aside. "There's a problem with the plywood we laid down yesterday."

Walker froze in the act of setting the tea in front of his wife. "What's wrong?"

"It won't hold up construction more than a few days," Sierra began. "But the plywood wasn't what we ordered. It was a lot thinner. One of the carpenters put his foot through a piece this morning."

"Was he hurt?" Walker asked sharply.

"No, he's fine. But when we pulled up the boards, we realized they weren't up to spec."

Walker drummed his fingers on the table. "Didn't anyone check the plywood when it was delivered?"

"Mark did." She should have checked, as well. "He said it was fine."

"Cameron came highly recommended. He's supposed to be the best."

"He'll figure it out. We've reordered from the lumberyard, and it should be delivered tomorrow. We'll get the floor relaid by the next day."

"This is an amateur mistake, Sierra." Walker frowned at her.

She knew it was. It wasn't clear who was at fault, but she was in charge, so it was her responsibility. She wasn't about to throw Mark under the bus. She'd personally check every piece of plywood in the next batch. "It won't happen again."

The doorbell rang, and Walker stood. "I'll get it."

Sierra heard the low rumble of men's voices at the front of the house. She couldn't distinguish their words, but a frisson of unease chased up her spine.

Jen leaned forward. "Are you sure this will only take a few days? I can't wait to get out of this house."

"Yes, I am. And we can make it up somewhere else." She'd make sure of it, even if everyone had to work overtime.

Sierra took a drink of her tea as Walker's visitor continued talking. People from town had stopped by other times she'd been at their house, but this voice didn't sound like the others.

It was flat. A little harder. As if business was being discussed.

Walker began speaking, and Sierra turned to Jen. "I know you're anxious to move in, and we'll do our best to make it happen quickly."

Jen waved at the kitchen walls. "We rented this place before we got married, and it's just too small for the four of us. I'm always tripping over Tommy's baseball stuff, and I swear that Nick's computer equipment reproduces at night. Every day there's more of it on the dining room table." She smiled. "Although I suspect Walker has a hand in that."

Sierra had met the two boys, and liked them both. The older one looked like Jen, and oddly enough, even Walker a little, with his blond hair and light eyes. The younger boy, Tommy, had dark hair and dark eyes. Sierra assumed he looked like his father.

Before she could respond, footsteps approached the kitchen. She glanced up, expecting to see Walker.

Nick Boone walked into the room.

She froze in her chair.

He stood studying her for a long moment, and hope sprang to life. Had he come to tell her he'd changed his mind? That he wanted to be part of his child's life?

One look at his hard, distant expression told her otherwise. "What are you doing here?" she asked.

"We have some unfinished business. And I don't mean the client you stole from me. I've already discussed that with Barnes, although I'm glad he gave you a job. Glad he gave me the means to track you down."

Walker stood behind Nick, his mouth compressed into a thin line, but there was no guilt in his expression. He hadn't told her old boss she was here.

Nick loomed above her, but she refused to feel cowed. "There's nothing between us. Business or otherwise."

It was hard to miss the relief that filled his eyes. It crushed the last stubborn speck of hope inside her. Beneath the edge of the table, she smoothed the soft knit material of her maternity shirt. "Have a good drive back to Chicago."

"You think I drove for five hours so you could blow me off? I'm not going anywhere until we've talked."

Instead of answering, she opened her notebook and began writing down what needed to be done at the construction site that day. Nick was still standing above her.

Watching her. She pressed too hard on the pen, and a tiny rip appeared in the thin paper.

"Sierra, do you want Boone to leave?" Walker still stood behind Nick, and even though he was a little shorter, a little leaner than the other man, he gave off a barely suppressed menace that was intimidating. "Do you want me to get rid of him?"

Her face felt as if it were cracking, but she managed a smile. "Thanks, Walker, but we're fine. I can deal with Nick." She focused on her client rather than her ex-boss as equal parts anger and pain slashed through her. Why had he come here?

Jen stood up and took Walker's arm. "We'll leave you to your business. Keep us updated on the wood situation, Sierra." She paused. "Yell if you need us," she added, staring at Sierra until she nodded.

Neither she nor Nick spoke as they listened to two sets of footsteps heading up the stairs. A door closed in the distance.

Sierra picked up the pen again and scribbled in her notebook until Nick put his hand over hers and stilled her fingers. "May I sit down?"

His hand was hot and brought back memories she wanted to forget. She yanked her arm away from him. "Go ahead, but there's no point. I have nothing to say to you."

"I have some things I need to say to you." He slid into the seat across the table. "I need to apologize."

She folded her hands on the table and met his gaze.

The remorse in his eyes surprised her, and she laid the pen carefully on the table. "For what, specifically?"

"You said there's nothing between us anymore, and I'm grateful. Relieved. But I still owe you an apology for the way I acted that night."

He thought she'd had an abortion.

Her throat tightened until she wasn't sure she could still breathe. She had no idea a few words could hurt so much. "You need to leave."

"Not until I've said what I have to say." Flags of red stained his cheekbones, and she knew this was hard for him. Nick was too controlled, too careful to make the kinds of mistakes that required detailed apologies.

"Fine. Say it, then go."

"I acted badly. Said things I regret. Please forgive me."

She closed her eyes briefly at his empty words, then forced herself to face him. "Do you really think it's that easy? That 'I'm sorry' makes everything right?" Her folded-together fingers pressed into the backs of her hands until they hurt. "What you said and did that night was unforgivable. What you said just now was worse. You won't find any absolution with me, Nick. But you can leave knowing you tried. I'm sure that will satisfy your conscience."

He pulled a folded check from the inside pocket of his jacket. "You wouldn't take this before. But you need it. For your expenses."

She grabbed the check and tore it to shreds. "Do you think money can fix everything? It can't fix this. I don't want your money. I don't want your apologies. I don't want anything from you." She shoved her chair back, pushing the table with enough force that it hit him in the stomach.

He stared at the small swell of her belly, plainly visible beneath the clingy material of her shirt. He paled. "You didn't…"

Her back was against the kitchen wall, the torn piece of wallpaper scratching at her ear. When she realized she'd pressed both hands to her bump, as if protecting her baby, she let her hands fall away. "No. I didn't."

"That changes everything."

"Not for you. I don't want to see you again. Is that clear?"

"It doesn't matter what you want," he said. His gaze drifted to her middle, then jerked back to her face. "I have responsibilities. Obligations. I understand that now."

He understood nothing—not the pain he'd inflicted, or the rage that made her want to bloody him. Not the hollow spot he'd carved out of her heart. "You have only the responsibilities and obligations that I allow you to have. That will be precisely none."

"I'm trying to do the right thing, Sierra."

"Too late. Way too late. At this point, the right thing is to turn around, walk away and forget about me and this baby."

"I'm not going to do that."

She came out from behind the table and pushed his chest, forcing him backward. Toward the front door.

"What are you going to do, Nick? Sue me for custody? Raise the baby yourself?"

He tried to control the flinch, but she saw it. "That's what I thought." She shoved him again, harder, through the kitchen door and into the dining room. "You need to leave."

He stepped back before she could touch him again. "I'll leave, but I'm not going away, Sierra. I'll talk to you again when you're more rational."

She flung open the front door and it bounced against the wall. As soon as he stepped out she shut it behind him.

With her spine pressed against it, she listened for signs that he'd left. He was still there, on the other side of the heavy wood. She could feel him, waiting for her to change her mind and open the door.

She didn't move until his footsteps retreated down the steps and his car engine roared to life, the tires squealing as he drove away.

Apparently, Nick had misplaced his famous control.

She returned to the kitchen, collected her belongings and let herself out the front door. She didn't want to face Jen and Walker. She didn't want to see the pity in their eyes, or the sympathy. Right now, kindness would make her fall apart.

She hadn't planned on telling anyone that Nick was the father of her baby, although Walker and Jen probably suspected, after he'd driven from Chicago to confront her. Having to face them now would be mortifying. She would be that tired, lame cliché, the woman who'd slept with her boss.

Sierra had run from Chicago to Otter Tail, but she wasn't going to run again. Standing on the porch, she took a deep, steadying breath, then another. The scent of lilacs followed her down the stairs, and the huge bushes next to the house, heavy with white and purple blossoms, bent in the breeze. Their scent filled the air— the smell of spring. Of hope.

Later this afternoon, she would cut some blossoms and bring them back to her apartment. She needed all the hope she could get right now.

CHAPTER SEVEN

NICK HAD TO GET AWAY. From Sierra. From that lump beneath her shirt.

From the contempt in her expression.

The tires of his Porsche squealed as he turned the corner too fast, and he forced himself to slow down. This was a small town. There would be pedestrians. Maybe dogs and cats running loose. He needed to be careful.

He drove up and down the narrow streets until his heart rate steadied and his breathing slowed, paying no attention to the houses and stores he passed. She'd been so angry. He'd assumed, after having time to think, she would want his help. That she'd be glad he understood that he had responsibilities.

He'd just made her more furious.

More devastated than she'd been the night she'd told him she was pregnant.

What was her problem? He was offering to help.

He didn't understand why she'd gotten so upset.

What the hell was he supposed to do now?

He slid into a parking spot between a battered, dark blue pickup truck and an older SUV, and scrubbed his hands over his still-hot face. She'd shoved him out the door as if the sight of him was unbearable. She'd said she never wanted to see him again, and she'd meant it.

How was he supposed to do the right thing if she wouldn't let him?

He had the rest of the weekend. They'd talk again.

The sun was beating down on the roof of the car, heating the interior. He got out and locked the door, then began walking.

He was in the business district of town. There were a couple of long streets, a couple of shorter, intersecting ones, and that was about it. The buildings were older, stretches of glass-fronted stores with decorative wood trim, and offices or apartments above them. About half were businesses he'd expect to see in a small town in northern Wisconsin—an ancient-looking barbershop, including a pole with washed-out colors, a bait and tackle store, a hardware store with faded merchandise behind dusty windows.

But there were newer looking places, as well. One of them, a restaurant called The Summer House, looked as trendy and inviting as anything in Chicago. He tried the door, but it was locked.

He continued walking, automatically cataloging the shops, assessing the mix of typical, dated architecture and more interesting rehabbed buildings. The town was in the middle of a face-lift.

When he realized he was sizing up the place with his architect's eyes, thinking about possibilities, he shoved his hands into the pockets of his slacks. He didn't give a damn about this town. He was here for one thing only. As soon as he got Sierra to see reason, he was going back to Chicago.

What did he want from her?

He wanted her to take his money so his conscience would be appeased. It was…all he could offer.

She didn't want his money. She'd said she didn't want anything from him.

She'd told him to leave. Walk away and forget about her and the baby.

He couldn't do that. That baby was his responsibility, and he'd make sure Sierra had enough money to take care of it.

Nick had to find a solution. It was like a puzzle, and he was good at them. He knew how to fit pieces together, how to come up with the answer.

Instead of the intricate design of a building, he would concentrate on solving Sierra.

Without noticing, he'd come to the end of the block. On the other side of the street, past an empty lot, he spotted a pub. The Harp and Halo. Maybe he'd have something to eat and regroup.

He stepped out of the shadows of the business district and into blinding sunshine and a gusting wind off the lake. The air held a faint, fishy odor and the smell of vegetation. Seaweed, maybe? He couldn't remember smelling anything like that at home.

In Chicago, the lake was more distant. It was a slice of beautiful blue from his office window, a curl of beige sand and green waves from his condo balcony. It was part of life in the city, but it wasn't in your face, the way it was in this town. Chicago was famous for its lakefront, but you could choose not to interact with it.

Not here. The smell of water permeated the air. The sound of it would be a constant companion. Even several blocks away from the shoreline, he'd heard the steady roll of waves hitting the beach.

It was a reminder that not everything could be controlled. That the lake would do what it liked, when it liked.

He hated it.

Yanking open the door to the pub, he stepped inside to a cool dimness and the faint smell of beer. There was no one else in the place, but a man stood behind the bar, polishing pint glasses. Nick slid onto one of the stools.

"Hi," he said to the bartender. "I'd like a beer, please."

The man put down the glass and towel. "Sorry, but we don't open until four." The dark-haired guy studied him for a moment, then lifted a pot of coffee out of the machine. "You look like you can use a cup of this, though."

Nick had rushed out of the tiny motel room this morning, determined to find Sierra and get the chore over with. He hadn't bothered to have breakfast before going to Walker Barnes's house. Maybe some caffeine would help unravel the tangle in his brain. He didn't like confusion. He wanted to see a clear path in front of him. He wanted a plan. "I could. Thanks."

The bartender poured a mug and set it on the green marble surface. "Cream? Sugar?"

"Black is fine." He took a sip and raised his eyebrows. "Great coffee."

"My wife is in charge of it. I'll pass the compliment along."

The bartender was tall and muscular, with dark hair that was a little too long. He would have been intimidating if his T-shirt hadn't read The Road to Hell is Paved with Adverbs.

Nick nodded at the shirt. "I like that. Are you a writer?"

He smiled, and Nick wondered why he'd thought the guy was intimidating. "My wife is a reporter." He held out his hand. "Quinn Murphy. Welcome to the Harp."

"Nick Boone," he replied, shaking hands. "Do you always serve coffee to people who wander in before you're open?" It was so different from Chicago that he might have stumbled into an alternate universe.

Murphy shrugged. "Why not? I'm here. I don't mind the company." He picked up the towel and another glass and began polishing again. "You visiting someone in town?"

Nick took a gulp of the coffee and it burned all the way to his stomach. "Trying to."

Murphy raised his eyebrows. "Sounds like a story there."

When Nick found himself on the verge of telling

this stranger what had happened this morning, he set the coffee down carefully. "A boring one. Thanks for the coffee. I appreciate it."

"No problem. Come back tonight, if you like. Our most popular band is playing."

Nick remembered all the pickup trucks he'd seen in town. "Thanks, but I'm not a big country music fan."

Murphy laughed. "What city are you from?" he asked.

"Chicago. Why?"

"Come back tonight. You need to have your preconceptions about small towns adjusted."

What the hell. Nick didn't have anything better to do. "Maybe I will."

SIERRA CLENCHED HER JAW as she left the lumberyard a half hour later. The foreman had insisted he'd delivered exactly what the specs had called for. She knew they hadn't—the plywood they'd ripped off this morning was a half inch thinner than it was supposed to be. Mark better be in his office—and he'd better have an explanation.

The drive-through line at the fast-food restaurant she passed was out into the street, so instead of pulling in, she kept going. She wanted answers more than she wanted to eat. Mark's office was several miles out of town, and she drove a little too fast on her way there.

As she pulled up to the log cabin that held his office, her back was sticky with sweat and her stomach churned. Not stopping to eat was a mistake—she was so hungry that she was afraid her stomach would growl during their meeting. She ate the crackers she kept in her purse, then hurried into the office.

After the cramped trailer on the construction site, she appreciated the simplicity and openness of Mark's office. A large chart that looked like a topographic map of Door County filled one wall. Metal filing cases stood beneath it, and three bare-bones metal desks were arranged against the other walls. Kyle, Mark's younger brother, who was one of the carpenters on her project, sat at the desk in the far corner. Mark was at the desk closest to the door.

"Hey, Sierra," he said. He was younger than she'd originally expected him to be, probably only in his early thirties, but he'd seemed knowledgeable. He'd had great recommendations.

His short, dark hair was messy, as if he'd run his fingers through it more than once. A tiny bit of mud clung to his boots, and his worn jeans were powdered with sawdust.

Six months ago, she probably would have felt a spark of interest in Mark. Today, she hoped she didn't embarrass herself during their meeting by needing to run to the bathroom.

"So what's up, Mark? How did this happen?" She dropped into a chair next to his desk.

He sighed. "After we pulled up all the plywood, I looked at every piece. Some of them were the right size, but the majority were quarter inch. Someone at the lumberyard must have accidentally mixed them together when they made up the order."

"Accidentally?" She raised her eyebrows.

Mark shook his head. "I've known the foreman for years and worked with him on dozens of projects. Vern wouldn't do this deliberately."

She'd reserve judgment on that. Vern had promised to talk to everyone involved in putting the order together, and she would see what he came up with. "This is a big problem."

"Not that big. Our insurance and the lumberyard's will cover the replacement of the wood. Vern promised he'd deliver it tomorrow."

"It's a problem because I had to tell Walker and Jen that I screwed up. I'm on shaky ground, anyway."

Mark glanced at her abdomen. "They can't blame your, ah, condition for this."

"They can say I was distracted," she retorted. "That I'm not giving the job my complete attention. Everything about that project is my responsibility. They're paying me to make sure stuff like this doesn't happen."

"We'll get to the bottom of it," Mark said wearily. He glanced at his brother. "Kyle and I are both working on it."

"Walker wants an explanation. And so do I."

"God," Mark muttered. "You look so nice. So normal. I never would have guessed you'd be a ball buster."

"Looks can be deceiving." Take Nick—he looked like a pillar of responsibility. "We can't have any more screw-ups," she said, slumping back in the chair. "Jen is in a hurry to get into this house."

"We won't have any. I'll pay more attention."

She nodded. "I will, too." As she stood up, hunger became queasiness. The morning sickness had faded in the last few weeks, but her friend Callie, as well as the OB-GYN she'd seen in Chicago, had warned her that she needed to eat regularly. Suddenly desperate to get back to her apartment, Sierra said, "I'll see you tomorrow at the job site."

"I'll be there."

As she reached the end of the driveway, she hesitated. The site was closer than the apartment. And she had a stash of Luna nutrition bars in her desk drawer. She could save time and get back to work more quickly by going to the site instead of home. A caramel chocolate brownie bar would hold her for a few hours.

Pleased with her efficient plan, she turned left instead of right. But after driving only a few minutes on the deserted country road, she had to pull over to the shoulder. Afraid to open the door into traffic, she barely managed to scramble over the console and open the door on the passenger side before she was sick.

She rinsed her mouth with the bottle of now-tepid water she'd left in the car, then leaned against the back of the seat. The scent of leather upholstery soothed her, and her eyes fluttered closed. She would drive to the site—and her stash of nutrition bars—in a minute. But she'd wait until her head stopped pounding and her stomach settled.

The sun warmed the interior of the car, and birds chirped in the trees alongside the road. The apple trees were finished blooming, but some blossoms still clung to a few branches, and their scent drifted in through the open door. She was so tired….

The sound of her name woke her from a deep sleep and became part of her dream. She was hiding in her office at Boone and Associates. She couldn't let Nick find her. She crawled under the desk, but heard her name again.

"Sierra. Sierra! Are you all right? What happened?"

Someone touched her shoulder and she startled awake. When she opened her eyes, Nick was leaning over her.

CHAPTER EIGHT

"Nick." *HE WAS TOO close*. The vestiges of her dream echoed in her head, and she scrambled to sit up. "What are you doing here?"

"What are *you* doing here, sleeping in your car on the side of the road? With the passenger door wide open." He frowned down at her, his face inches from hers.

The dream retreated, leaving her feeling vulnerable and horribly off balance. Needing to get away from him. "You should watch where you stand," she said. "I was sick."

He stepped back, and when he was clear of the door, she pulled it closed, then lifted herself over the console and into the driver's seat. But before she could drive away, he yanked open the passenger door again and slid into the vehicle.

In the small front seat, his shoulders looked very broad, his chest heavily muscled. He'd exchanged his slacks and dress shirt for jeans and a red polo. He smelled of the outdoors, and heat rolled off him in waves. "Get out of my car, Nick."

"You say you're sick and you think I'm going to walk away?"

"That's exactly what I think. I'm fine now."

His arms were lean, with fine dark hairs, and his skin gleamed with sweat. She hadn't seen him in short sleeves very often—he always wore dress shirts to work. When she found herself staring at them, remembering the feel of his arms around her, she jerked her gaze away and focused on a small bird sitting on the barbed wire fence in front of her.

Foolish to think about Nick that way. Stupid. He had startled her, that was all. When she was wide awake, she wanted nothing to do with him.

"Sierra, I'm worried about you. What's going on?"

He clearly wasn't going to leave until she told him what had happened, and it was too hot in the car to argue about it. She rolled the window down. "I was queasy. I pulled over and got sick, then closed my eyes for a moment. I guess I fell asleep." She turned the key in the ignition and the SUV rumbled beneath her as she shifted into Drive. "Get out of my car, Nick."

"Do you have the flu? Food poisoning?"

"Oh, for God's sake." She shoved the gearshift back into Park. "You can't be that ignorant about pregnancy. It's called morning sickness. Pregnant women get it. Or haven't you ever seen any movies or read any books?"

"Of course I have. But it's the middle of the afternoon."

"'Morning' sickness isn't literal," she muttered. "It can be anytime. I got sick and now I'm better. So you can go."

When he didn't get out of the car, she swiveled to

face him. "You think I can't push you out the car door? Try me."

"I'm worried, Sierra. Smart women don't sleep along the side of a country road with the door open unless something is wrong."

The baby chose that moment to move, and she put her palm over her abdomen. She'd been able to feel it moving for the past week, and it still seemed like a miracle.

He stared at her hand. "What? What's wrong? Are you feeling sick again?"

She let her arm drop away. "What are you talking about?"

"You were holding your stomach."

She skimmed her hand over the slight bulge again and despite her anger with Nick, her mouth softened into a tiny smile. "My baby was moving. I never get tired of feeling it."

He frowned as he studied the lump beneath the light blue shirt. "What does it feel like?"

That was the first question he'd asked about her pregnancy. About the baby. Sierra wanted to ignore him, but it was his baby, too. "It's just a little flutter at this point. Why do you want to know?"

"Just curious." He peered at her abdomen, as if waiting to see her skin ripple. "Something moving inside you makes me think of that thing from the *Alien* movies."

"*Alien?* That's charming." So much for getting warm and fuzzy with Nick about the baby.

"That's the view from the other chromosome. I've

never been around a pregnant woman. I don't know anything about being pregnant."

"And you don't want to know."

"I never did before." His mouth flattened. "I do now. This wasn't my choice, but I want to do the right thing, Sierra."

"And how do you define that?"

"I have no idea. Whatever you want me to do."

"The right thing is to leave me alone and forget about us." She and the baby were already an *us*. A unit.

"I won't do that. I have an obligation to you." He gestured toward the bump. "You didn't make that by yourself."

"But I'm going to deal with *my baby* by myself. You've already made it clear how you feel about the situation, and that suits me perfectly. We don't need you."

"That's not your choice. I don't want attachments, and I've never made a secret of that. I still don't, but it's too late now. There's going to be a baby, and I'm responsible." He shifted in his seat so he faced her. "I won't back down on that."

It felt as if he were digging a knife into her heart. "I know you're very conscientious about your duties. About fulfilling your responsibilities. It was one of the things I admired about you. Now it's just annoying. I don't want you hanging around, pissed off because I chose to have the baby, trying to figure out how to do the 'right thing'." She mimed quotation marks in the air. "Your sense of duty is a problem for both of us."

"Is that why you're so angry? Because you think I wanted you to have an abortion?"

"I saw your face this morning when you thought I had. You were relieved. Happy." She gripped the steering wheel and watched a cardinal land on a branch and flick its tail.

"It would have been easier."

She had to give him credit for being honest. "For both of us. But that's not a choice I'm going to make."

"Then we deal with reality. The baby is half mine. You chose to have it, and I'm going to take responsibility for my part. You can't make that decision for me."

He'd get tired of seeing to his *responsibilities*. "I don't know what you think you can do from Chicago."

"I can send money from Chicago. Or you could move back."

"Adjust my life for you? Why would I do that? I have a job here. I've made promises."

"Then we'll have to figure out a way for this to work, won't we?"

Time to change the subject, because arguing with him was like beating her head against a rock. "What are you doing out here, anyway?"

"I was on my way to your job site. After I left his house, I called Barnes, and he told me about your problem. I thought, since I was here anyway, there might be something I could do to help."

Territoriality stirred, but she tried to ignore it. "Thank you," she said, resting against the door as she faced him. "That's not necessary, but it's very generous of you."

Regardless of what was between them personally, Nick was a good architect. "But unless you can read minds and go back into the past, there's nothing you can do. Someone made a mistake, and we have to figure out how it happened."

"Are you sure it wasn't deliberate?" He leaned against the other door.

God, she hoped not. It meant someone she was working with was trying to cheat her. "Mark swears that the foreman of the lumberyard is honest. He's worked with him many times before this."

Nick's forehead wrinkled in a frown. "Mark is...?"

"The general contractor. Walker did the research and chose him. He came highly recommended."

"Check everything yourself from now on," Nick said, straightening. "Don't trust anyone else to do it."

"Believe me, I won't." She pushed away from the door and sat up. "I know how to handle this. It's not the first project I've worked on."

"It's the first time you've been on your own."

"Are you implying I don't know what I'm doing? That this mistake was somehow my fault?" Her hands closed into fists. "Why did you call Walker, anyway? Were you trying to get him to give the project back to you?"

"Of course not." Nick shifted in the seat and glanced out the window. Following his gaze, she saw that another bird had joined the cardinal on the fence. It looked similar, but it was brown instead of red.

"Why, then?"

"I wanted to know where the site was," he finally said. "So I knew where to find you."

"You would have come to my workplace?" she asked carefully.

"If necessary." He held her gaze. "I'm serious about this baby thing. Money may be all I can give you, but I *will* give you that." He leaned a little closer. "You can be as self-righteous as you want, but why would you refuse money for your kid?"

Her kid. Not theirs. But he had a point. She didn't have the right to refuse a gift to her child. "Fine, Nick. I'll think about what you said. About what I want to do about it. That's all I can promise."

"That's enough for now." He opened the door and stepped out of her car, then hesitated. "You're not going to the job site now, after being sick, are you? Do you want me to follow you home?"

"I'm fine, and I have work to do. Goodbye, Nick."

"I'll see you again before I leave town," he said, closing the door.

"You're staying here?"

"Yeah, at the Bide-a-Wee Motel on the other side of town."

The same place she'd stayed. It was in the middle of nowhere, with just-plowed fields on one side and black-and-white cows grazing on the other.

"Not for long, I'm guessing. I figure you'll be bored out of your mind by ten o'clock tomorrow morning." She gripped the steering wheel more tightly. "Maybe sooner. I won't be offended if you decide to leave town."

"I'm not going anywhere." He closed her door carefully and walked to a sleek black sports car parked a little behind her SUV on the other side of the road.

She'd seen Nick's ferocious concentration on every job he'd done. Damn it. He wasn't going to give up.

THE HARP AND HALO LOOKED like a different place when Nick walked in that evening. Instead of dim and quiet, it was packed with people. The clinking of glasses, the ripple of voices, occasional laughter filled the room. Energy crackled in the air, making the place feel alive. And it wasn't even seven o'clock yet. He wondered if all these people were here for the band, or if this was a typical Friday night.

He went to his share of exclusive clubs in Chicago—the women he dated expected to be taken to them. Those places were all about seeing and being seen, about wearing the right clothes and buying the right drinks.

Beer seemed to be the preferred beverage here, but there were a few glasses of wine and the occasional whiskey on the rocks. That was it.

Not a cosmopolitan or appletini in sight. That was refreshing, too.

The booths along the opposite wall and the tables down the middle of the room were all full. Three men and a slender blonde woman were setting up musical instruments at the front, but there was no music playing at the moment. Unlike the big city clubs, you could actually have a conversation in here.

Nick edged his way to the bar, and nodded at the bartender when he caught his eye.

"You came back," Murphy said with a smile. "Welcome. What can I get you?"

"What single malt scotches do you have?"

He pulled a piece of paper from beneath the bar. "Here you go."

There were several single malts listed, as well as a few varieties of Irish whiskey. "Impressive list," Nick said.

The bartender looked up from the beer he was pulling. "For a Podunk town?" he said, his eyes twinkling. "I like to surprise people."

"Surprised the hell out of me. Someone knows their whiskey."

"That would be me," Murphy said. "I used to have a deep and intimate acquaintance with it."

That was frank. "How about an eighteen-year Macallan?" Nick said, looking more carefully at the guy. "Straight up."

Murphy reached to a cabinet above the top shelf of bottles. "Good choice." He poured the amber liquid and set it carefully on a coaster, as if it were liquid gold. "Nineteen bucks."

Nick pushed some bills across the green marble surface and glanced at the unfamiliar names on the beer taps. "Next time I'm here, I'll try one of your beers."

"We have some good local craft choices. Come in when we're less busy and we can talk about them."

"Thanks. I will."

Murphy began to draw another beer, and as Nick edged through the crowd, he heard snippets of conversations all around him. One man was talking about his shift at the canning factory. A woman was leaning against another man, talking about what the kids had done that day. Another woman grumbled about her commute to Green Bay.

People greeted one another by name and drifted from one group to another. They were all connected, all familiar, all friends.

He passed through the crowd as if he were invisible, moving from one circle to the next. A stranger. When he caught someone's eye, the person would smile politely and return to his or her conversation. Nick was in a bubble of anonymity, and it was unsettling.

He'd never been part of a group of friends who met at a pub on a Friday night to have a beer and catch up. Never wanted to be. But this pub was welcoming. If he were into that new age stuff, he'd say it had a good vibe.

Nick wished he was part of it.

Which was stupid. He had nothing in common with these people. They wouldn't care about his life. But for a moment, he wanted to belong.

He sipped his scotch and eased between two tables. He was unsettled because of the situation with Sierra. That's all it was. He wasn't used to a woman telling him to take a hike. Especially one with whom he had such a close connection.

He'd had a close connection with the last woman who'd dumped him, too.

His mother.

Since then, he hadn't given any of them a chance. He was the one who said goodbye.

That wasn't an option with Sierra. He took another sip of scotch to burn away the expected rush of panic, but it never appeared.

She'd fascinated him from the beginning, although he'd been careful to keep his distance. Other than that night. And now she wanted nothing to do with him. Or his money.

As if he conjured her with his thoughts, he saw her dark red head at the table in the corner. She was sitting with Walker and Jen Barnes. A good-looking man was settled in close to Sierra. Nick tightened his grip on the scotch as he made his way toward their table.

"Sierra. Walker. Jen. How are you?"

The Barneses murmured hello. "Why don't you join us?" Jen asked.

Nick glanced at Sierra, who appeared frozen. He saw the struggle in her expression—if she said no, she'd have to explain why. Finally, she nodded once. "Yes, Nick. Pull up a chair." She turned to the man on her left. "This is Mark Cameron. He's the contractor for Jen and Walker's house."

He wasn't a date. Nick smiled as he reached across the table. "Good to meet you." He grabbed an empty chair at an adjoining table and wedged it between Sierra and Cameron.

"So," Nick said, taking another drink of scotch. "What have you found out about the plywood?"

CHAPTER NINE

THE CONVERSATIONS AROUND them, the clink of glasses, the rattle of silverware faded away as Nick sat down beside Sierra. He was too close—he'd squeezed in between her and Mark—and it was impossible to ignore him. She smelled the rich peat smoke of the whiskey he was drinking, the aftershave he always wore, the soap he'd used. His thigh was inches from hers, and heat crawled over her.

She wanted to edge away, but knew she couldn't. She'd seen the speculative expression on Jen's face when Nick strolled up. Sierra needed to avoid questions about her former boss.

So she plastered a smile on her face. When he asked what they'd found out about the plywood, she and Mark rehashed everything they'd just told Jen and Walker— they'd made no progress in figuring it out, but more had arrived, a rush delivery, and they'd checked every piece. The conversation drifted to other topics—normal business talk, the kind she'd had with Nick innumerable times.

There was nothing normal about this situation.

"You're moving along, then. Great." Nick turned to

Jen and Walker as he patted her hand. She eased away casually, as if his touch meant nothing. "You'll enjoy working with Sierra," he said. "She's the best associate I have." He smiled. "Had, I guess."

Walker stretched his legs out. "You're recommending Sierra for this job? You were singing a different tune this morning."

"Of course I was," Nick said easily. "This morning I was pissed off that I'd lost the project. I'm still not happy about it—I'd like to have your house in my portfolio. But if I can't do it, I'm glad Sierra is going to."

"That's generous of you," Jen said. Her eyes narrowed just a little as she studied Nick. Sierra guessed that not too many people conned Jen.

Nick shrugged. "Sierra is a good architect. I'm hoping if I play nice, she'll come back to Boone and Associates when she finishes this job."

He laid his arm along the back of her chair. The gesture meant nothing—he'd done it before in meetings, no matter who was sitting next to him. She'd never paid any attention.

Tonight, her skin burned with awareness. It felt as if he was spinning a web around her, drawing her closer and closer. She pushed her chair back abruptly and his arm fell away. "Excuse me for a moment," she said, snatching up her purse.

As the restroom door whooshed closed behind her, Sierra stared at herself in the mirror. Her eyes were too bright and her skin was flushed.

She couldn't let Nick see he affected her.

She straightened her shirt and swiped her damp palms down her thighs. He'd use any opening she gave him, and she wasn't going to give him that opportunity.

Sierra splashed cold water on her face, smoothed down her hair, reapplied her lip gloss. When her pulse had steadied and she felt calm again, she returned to the table. As she sat down, she managed to slide her chair away from Nick's. If he noticed, he didn't react.

He was busy discussing the project with Walker and Mark. *Her* project. All three of them were leaning forward, elbows on the table, talking about drainage fields and solar shingles and insulation.

"Have you solved all my problems?" she said sarcastically as she scooted her chair closer. She glanced at Nick. "I hope so. It's always nice to get free advice."

Jen hid a tiny smile behind her soda glass.

"Working on it," Nick answered. "Give us another hour or two, and we'll have that house built and landscaped."

"You're welcome to the landscaping," she said to him. "That's not my area of expertise." She drained her ginger ale and beat back a wave of weariness. Suddenly, she wanted nothing more than to fall into bed and sleep for the rest of the night.

But leaving now wasn't an option. It would be a sign of weakness, and this was business. She'd learned early in architecture school that women in the men's world of construction and building couldn't be polite and courteous. They had to speak up, interrupt the same way the men did, push their agenda forcefully.

So she waded into the discussion, trading ideas with Mark and Nick, listening to Jen's and Walker's thoughts. When the band struck their first notes, everyone stopped talking and she settled against the back of her chair. Thank goodness. She could listen to a few songs, then say good-night.

"One last thing," Nick said, raising his voice to be heard over the music. "If you need a second opinion on anything, any help, let me know." He turned to her and nudged her shoulder. "Sierra and I have always worked well together."

She kicked him in the ankle and he moved his shoulder. "This is a little far to go for a casual consultation, isn't it?" she asked.

He held her gaze for a moment, then smiled easily at Jen and Walker. "I'll be back. I like this town. There's a lot going on up here."

"Really?" Sierra raised her eyebrows. "I didn't realize you were such a fan of cows."

"Big one," he assured her. "I found some excellent cheese in a little store along County S. I've developed a whole new appreciation for them."

"You're going to become a cheesehead? You'd look good in one of those cheddar wedge hats."

He grinned at her. "You think so? I'll keep my eyes open for one."

She had to go. Anger and exhaustion were making her reckless, and Jen was watching her and Nick with fascinated interest. A few more back and forths, and Jen would know something was going on with them.

Sierra stood and smiled at everyone at the table. "Good night, all. I have an appointment bright and early tomorrow."

"We're not slave drivers," Walker said. "You don't have to work on Saturday."

This wasn't work related—she was having her first ultrasound. "Just a few things I need to take care of," she said lightly. "It won't take long."

She slung her purse over her shoulder and wove through the tables. The band launched into their next song, "Natural Woman," and she was almost to the door when the drummer began to sing.

Delaney had an amazing voice. Sierra moved to the side of the bar to listen for a few moments, and Nick came up beside her.

Damn it. He'd think she had waited for him.

But he was staring at the musicians. "No wonder everyone told me to come and listen to the band tonight," he said. He glanced at her. "Sure you don't want to stay and listen for a while?"

"I can't," she said. "But you enjoy them." Leaving him behind, she pushed through the door and into the dusk. Purple shadows painted the downtown, and the streetlights had turned on. The wind carried the fresh scent of the lake again, and she heard the distant thunder of waves against rocks. She loved having the lake close by, and it hadn't taken long for her to get used to the sound. The repetitive roll and crash rocked her to sleep, reassured her when she woke in the middle of the night.

She hadn't expected to become so familiar with it so quickly. She'd thought the lack of street noise would bother her. In Chicago, it was traffic sounds that drifted in her window, even in the high-rise condo. Horns beeping, engines gunning, police and fire sirens, the rumble of passing buses all blended together in a reassuring mosaic. Familiar. Comforting. The sounds of home.

This was her home now, at least for the next several months.

Pulling on her sweater, she started down the street.

The door of the pub opened behind her, and the tingle at the back of her neck told her who it was. She walked a little faster, but he caught up easily. "Do you need a ride home?" Nick asked.

"No, thank you. I prefer to walk." As she turned the corner, a cold spring wind off the lake pushed at her back, whipping her hair into her face and slicing through the thin material of her sweater. She hunched her shoulders and pulled it more tightly around her.

Nick settled his leather jacket around her shoulders, and his scent drifted up from it. She tried to shrug it off, but he put his hand on her back. "Leave it. You're cold."

She glanced at his short-sleeved cotton shirt. "You will be, too."

"I'm fine."

Finally she met his gaze, her hands going to her hips in anger. "What are you trying to do, Nick?"

"What do you mean?"

"All this friendliness, joining our table, talking

shop with Mark and Walker. Offering your help. Are you trying to undermine me? Are you hoping Walker gives the project back to you?" After their earlier conversation, the thought had simmered in her head all evening.

He stopped walking and stared at her. "Do you really think I'd do that? Even though you took the job away from me, I wouldn't take it back if he offered. Not now."

"I don't know what you'd do." Without thinking, she drew the jacket closer and huddled into its comfort. "But I know you're planning something. I know how you think. You're always four steps ahead of everyone else." She glanced at him again. "That's why you're so successful."

"I'm hearing a 'but'," he said.

"But this time, it's pissing me off. You're trying to sneak into my life sideways."

"Yes, I am, because you've given me no choice. That's my baby." He pointed at her abdomen. "I'm going to be part of this."

"I told you we're not your responsibility or obligation."

"You said you'd think about it," he corrected. "I'm making my case that I'll do whatever it takes."

She turned the final corner. Her apartment was halfway down the street, and she walked a little faster. She didn't want to fight with him tonight. Exhaustion was sucking all the energy from her body and making her legs feel like stone. If she continued this conversation, she would say or do something she'd regret later. Weariness had weakened her normal barriers.

He fell into step beside her, but she ignored him. She was surprised when he didn't say anything, either. When she glanced at him, his cheeks and ears were red and his shoulders tensed against the wind.

She slipped into the tiny vestibule next door to The Summer House, Jen's restaurant. Nick shouldered his way in behind her as she fumbled in her purse for the key to the glass door at the bottom of the stairs. When she got it open, she turned to face him.

"This is where I live. Good night, Nick."

"May I come in with you for a few minutes?" He took the door and held it open for her. "I think we need to continue this conversation."

"Not tonight," she said. "I'm too tired to deal with you." She didn't want him in her space, looking at her things, filling the small living room with his presence.

He gazed at her steadily, and she had no trouble reading his expression. If she didn't let him in, he wouldn't turn around and leave. He'd wait outside her door. Making it impossible to sleep, knowing he was there.

Why did she still care about him when he was behaving so badly? She was too tired to think about that.

"Fine. Come on up."

She trudged up the stairs, each step a huge effort. Thank goodness she didn't have to work tomorrow. She could sleep in. She had nowhere to be until her ultrasound appointment at 11:00 a.m.

Nick followed, staying close behind as if he was afraid she'd change her mind before he got into her apartment. When she unlocked the door at the top of the stairs, warm air scented with vanilla and butter drifted out.

"Smells good," he said, as she stepped aside and he walked in. "Were you baking?"

"It's from the restaurant downstairs."

"I noticed that place earlier. Is it any good?"

"It's Jen's restaurant. And it's wonderful." Sierra handed him his jacket, already missing its warmth. She turned up the heat, then waved him into the room. "Have a seat."

He wandered over to the built-in bookshelves and studied her collection of photographs—pictures of her with her mother and father, her friends from college, Callie and the rest of the people she hung out with in Chicago. Sierra shut the blinds on the windows that overlooked the street. She turned on the lamps sitting on the old mahogany end tables, then flicked on the light attached to the ceiling fan. She wanted the room bright and businesslike.

She sank into the red chair and watched him catalog her apartment. As he wandered, she used her foot to smooth out the rag rug covering the scuffed hardwood floors.

Finally he turned. "Nice place," he said.

"It's comfortable." She had never seen where he lived, but she was sure it made this tiny apartment look completely shabby. She gestured toward the couch. "Don't bother to try and intimidate me by standing there and staring down at me. I'm too tired to play those games. Sit down."

"Intimidate you?" He sank onto the couch, resting against her mother's multicolored afghan, folded over the back. "I'm not sure that's possible," he said. "I've seen you deal with everyone from admins to colleagues to hard-ass construction workers. None of them has ever rattled you."

"Trying to sweet-talk me now, Boone?"

A tiny smile appeared, quickly controlled. "Would it work?"

"Of course not." But she held his gaze a moment too long. When she felt herself weakening, she pulled her feet onto the cushion and wrapped her arms around her legs. "I'm beat. What was so important to talk about tonight?"

He shifted forward and rested his elbows on his knees. "I need to know what I can do to convince you to listen to me. To let me do what's right. How can I prove that I'm sincere? That I want to do this?"

She rose from the chair and went over to the bookcase to straighten a picture of herself with her parents. Her fingers lingered for a moment, then she turned back to Nick. "I know you're sincere. I know you want to do this. You take your obligations very seriously."

"Then what's the problem?"

She drew a deep breath and turned to face him. "You are, Nick. You're not the kind of man I want as my child's father."

"Too late to worry about that. I already am."

"Only biologically. Tell me, do you want to be involved in the baby's life? Share custody with me? Help raise him or her? Does your sense of responsibility extend past the day I give birth?"

He stood and moved closer. "I haven't thought that far ahead," he admitted.

"Pregnancy is temporary. Parenthood is forever. Are you prepared to be a parent?"

He stopped and shoved his hands into his pockets. "No," he finally said. "I'm not good father material."

His shoulders were tense, his jaw clenched. "Why is that, Nick?"

He walked over to the window and lifted a slat of the blinds to stare into the night. "Too many reasons to list. But I can do other things. I have plenty of money. I can make sure you have whatever you need."

"If I accept your money, I'd want you to be involved in the baby's life. You paid me a good salary when I worked for you, and I have a savings account." Things would be tight for a while. But she would manage. "But since you can't give me what I want, there's no point in talking about what you *can* give."

"What do you want, Sierra?" He turned to face her, but didn't move closer.

"I want my child to have the same thing I had when I was growing up—parents who love her."

"Her? You hope it's a girl?"

"Who make sure she knows they do," she continued, ignoring him. "Who think she hangs the moon and the stars. I won't let anyone, even my baby's father, make my child think she's a burden. An obligation. Nothing but a responsibility."

"I don't have to be involved in the kid's life to help you," he said. He sounded confused. He didn't understand.

"Let me spell it out, Nick." Sierra stepped closer to him and immediately regretted it. But she wasn't going to back away. "Babies become toddlers, then go to school, and it happens fast. My baby will make friends and meet her friends' fathers. She'll ask me why she doesn't have a dad. What am I supposed to tell her? He sends money, but he doesn't want anything to do with you?"

Nick flinched, but she continued speaking. "That's why it's best if you just leave now and forget about me and the baby. If you want to feel as if you've fulfilled your obligations, have your attorney set up a trust fund for college."

Don't get my hopes up that you could ever give more.

"Good night, Nick." She opened the door.

There was regret in his expression. Sadness? But he didn't deny what she'd said. Reality replaced hope in the bright, quiet room. Eventually, he walked out the door, and she shut it behind him.

CHAPTER TEN

Nick reached for the doorknob, hoping she would change her mind, but she'd already locked it. The light beneath the door went dark. Her footsteps headed to the back of the apartment.

Dismissing him.

She told him if he wanted her to accept his money, she expected him to be a part of the baby's life. When he couldn't agree, she'd walked away.

The narrow hallway smelled faintly of cleaning solution, sharp and acrid. They must be closing the restaurant downstairs. The hall was lit by a single lightbulb, which threw a distorted shadow of him against the wall. He sank onto the top step, hoping Sierra would return, open the door and tell him she would accept his money without expecting him to be a part of this baby's life. But there were no sounds of movement from the other side of the door. No lights turning back on.

He sat in the silence, fighting panic as he thought about the rounded curve beneath Sierra's shirt and what it meant. It wasn't just a pregnancy. That was a child. *His* child. If Sierra had her way, he would be tethered to it forever.

A child he might get attached to.

He stood abruptly and hurried down the stairs and out into the cool night air. The wind from the lake was strong, and scattered raindrops pelted the pavement. The swirls and gusts carried away Sierra's perfume, which had been clinging to his jacket. But no amount of wind and rain could wash away who he was.

He could try to be the man she wanted him to be. But she would see the truth eventually. That there was something missing inside him.

Sooner or later, she'd see that money was the only thing he could give her.

THE NEXT MORNING, AS he waited on the bench down the street from Sierra's apartment, Nick finished his coffee, while the second cup he'd bought for Sierra cooled. He crushed his cup and tossed it into the trash can.

Her coffee was completely cold by the time she emerged from her building. She was wearing a heavy sweater and another shirt that clung to the curve of her belly. He focused on her face instead of that lump as she came out the door.

She slowed when she saw him. "Nick. What are you doing here?"

"Waiting for you. I wanted to continue our conversation." He extended the cup of coffee. "It's cold, but I know you need coffee in the morning."

"Thank you, but I'm pretty full right now. Caffeine is off-limits, anyway."

He dumped it in the trash. "Then we'll just talk."

"Not now," she said as she began walking along the sidewalk. "I have an appointment."

"Forget the damn appointment. Barnes was right. This is Saturday. Take the day off."

"You know it's not like that in our business," she said, studying the smooth, even sidewalk as if she were picking her way across a minefield. "You meet people when they have free time."

"So who are you meeting today?"

She didn't answer until they'd reached the mouth of the alley. "It's not a business appointment," she finally said. "It's personal."

Was it Cameron? Nick clenched his jaw. Who else did she know in this town besides the Barneses? "Personal can wait."

"Not this time." She finally looked at him. "I'm having an ultrasound, Nick. I'm nineteen weeks pregnant, and the doctor told me to have this done."

"Why?" He grabbed her arm. "Is something wrong?"

"It's routine." She extracted herself from his grip. "Almost every pregnant woman has one at this point."

If he was going to try and make this right, it had to start now. "Okay. I'll come with you."

She went still. "Why?"

"You want me to get involved, I'm going to get involved. I'll drive you to the appointment."

"Really?" She watched him steadily. "Are you going

to watch the ultrasound, too? That's what expectant fathers do."

His stomach twisted, but he gave a sharp jerk of his head. "If you want me there."

She glanced down the alley, as if trying to decide whether to run or stay. Then she squared her shoulders. "You're right. This is what I said I wanted. So you can come with me."

He put his hand on her back and steered her toward his car, parked on the street. "Where are we going?"

"Sturgeon Falls." She pulled two sheets of paper out of her purse. "I have the directions."

"Good. You navigate. I'll drive." He glanced at her, reassured when he saw that she was just as uncertain about this as he was. "We've always made a good team."

FORTY-FIVE MINUTES LATER, he'd changed his mind. They might be a good team at the office. In their personal lives, it was another story.

Two other couples sat in the waiting room of the medical building. Both the women were huge. Sierra was going to look like that eventually, too.

Both men nodded at him. Acknowledging their shared condition. Nick swallowed once, then eased into the uncomfortable chair next to Sierra.

Before he'd had a chance to wrap his mind around what he was going to do, the nurse showed them into a room. Sierra went first. When she got to the door, she looked over her shoulder, waiting for him. Decision time.

He followed her in.

The woman handed Sierra a sheet and said, "Everything off below the waist. You can leave your socks on, though. It's cold in here."

The nurse closed the door, and even in the dimly lit room, he saw color rise in Sierra's face. "Go ahead," he said gruffly as he turned his back. "Unless you want me to leave."

"No, I'm fine." He heard one shoe drop to the floor, then the other. The rustle of denim being pulled down. A soft whisper of fabric following it.

What kind of underwear did a woman use when she was pregnant?

He had no idea what Sierra normally wore, other than the skimpy purple thing she'd had on that night. The one he'd almost had to remove for her.

When he felt his body stir, he closed his eyes. He was a bastard. She was thinking about her baby, and all he wanted to do was watch her undress.

Something crinkled and slid, and Sierra said, "I'm good. You can turn around."

She lay on the table, a paper sheet pulled above her waist, her shirt carefully draped over it and her sock-covered feet showing at the end. She worried her lower lip as she looked at the complicated machine next to the table, and he realized she was anxious.

"You okay?" he asked.

"I'm fine." She glanced at the machine again. "A little nervous, I guess. What if something's wrong?"

Without thinking, he took her hand. Instead of

pushing him away, she gripped hard and clung. Her fingers were ice-cold.

"Everything is fine." He took a step closer, until he was wedged between the bed and the wall. "You said this was routine."

"I know, but now I'm worried." She was still staring at the machine, and she sounded hoarse.

"Are you thirsty? Do you want some water?"

She glanced at him, and her mouth softened. "I would love a glass of water."

He found a stack of coffee cups on the counter and filled one with water, then handed it to her. She propped herself up on one elbow and drank it down. The sheet slipped a little, revealing a crescent of creamy skin, and he couldn't tear his gaze away. When she noticed him looking, she snatched the sheet higher, covering herself.

After disposing of the empty cup, he took her hand again. Her fingers curled around his, and after a moment, they weren't as cold.

A young woman walked into the room. "Hi, I'm Karen, the technician. I'll be doing your ultrasound today." She glanced from him to Sierra. "Is this your first one?"

"Yes," Sierra said. Her fingers clung to his more tightly.

"All you have to do is lie there," Karen said to her. She glanced at Nick and nodded at their joined hands. "You've already got your job covered."

She folded the sheet down, revealing the pale, curved

expanse of Sierra's belly. After squirting a clear gel on her skin, Karen put an instrument on the gel and started moving it around.

Sierra turned her head to watch the screen, but there was nothing to see. Just blackness, with a few wavy white lines. Then a tiny form came into view.

Its head looked too big for its body, but its arms and legs were moving. Although it was tiny, it looked like a baby.

Fragile.

Completely defenseless.

Nick wanted to back out of the room and run as fast as he could. Instead, he moved closer to Sierra.

As she stared at it, a tear rolled down her cheek. She touched the image on the screen, as if she was trying to hold it in her hand. She glanced up at him, and he saw the wonder in her expression. The joy.

Not what he was feeling.

Reality was a punch in the gut, and it left him unable to breathe. If he did what Sierra wanted, he'd be responsible for protecting it. Keeping it safe. Raising it.

He could think of nothing more terrifying.

He stood next to the table in the cold room, with Sierra still clinging to his hand, and watched the technician move the instrument around. It seemed as if she went over the same area again and again, stopping every few seconds to type into the machine. "Why do you keep doing that?" he asked. "Is something wrong?"

The young woman smiled at him. "No, I'm just

taking measurements. It's routine, Dad. Don't worry about it."

Dad. Oh, God, that's what he would be in a few months.

Sierra looked up at him, her eyes wary, her expression easy to read. She was afraid he was going to freak out. He wanted to. But he'd promised her he'd try to do this.

Seeing a tiny image on a screen wasn't going to make him break that promise. He squeezed her hand and tried to smile reassuringly. He must have succeeded, because she smiled back. Her mouth quivered and another tear rolled down her cheek. She held his gaze a moment too long, then turned back to the screen.

Her fingers slipped between his as she twined them together. More than comfort. Intimate. Connected. His impulse was to pull away. Instead, he ran his thumb over the back of her hand.

Finally, fifteen minutes later, the torture was over. The technician left the room and he let go of Sierra's hand. She slid off the table, the sheet wrapped around her waist, and he turned his back.

He heard the sounds in reverse—first her underwear, then her jeans, then shoes. More intimacy in an already unsettling day. Trying to ignore her, he visualized the plans for the building he was working on, concentrating on adding up numbers in his head.

It didn't help. He heard every breath she took in the quiet room. Every slight movement of clothing against skin. Before he turned back to Sierra, he shrugged his jacket on to hide his erection. She'd think he was a complete pig.

She'd be right.

Sierra didn't relax until the doctor came in and told her everything looked good and the baby was progressing normally. As they left the room, the technician returned and handed Sierra a piece of paper. She stared down at it, until curiosity made him look over her shoulder. It was a picture of the baby, in all its fragility.

"Next time, I'll probably be able to tell you the sex," the woman said cheerfully.

Next time? He had to do this again?

Nick didn't say anything as they walked to the car. He had to catch her elbow once, when she stumbled on a piece of broken pavement. She was too busy staring at the picture to watch where she was going.

As they drove back to Otter Tail, his sweaty hands were slippery on the steering wheel. He took a curve a little too fast, and pumped the brakes to slow them down.

"That freaked you out, didn't it?" Sierra said.

"I'm fine."

"I saw your face, Nick. You looked like you'd just been hit by a truck."

He'd felt that way, too. "I wasn't expecting to see the baby moving around. Looking so real."

"It was amazing," she said.

The awe in her voice made him grip the steering wheel harder. An abandoned orchard flashed past the window, the trees twisted and gnarled. Weeds grew knee-high beneath them, and the fence had fallen in places.

It would take a lot of work to make that orchard productive, and there was no guarantee the trees would even bear fruit again. He was like that orchard—too bent to be put right. Sierra might as well accept the truth.

Dad.

He couldn't be a father to her baby.

SIERRA GLANCED AT NICK as the car sped up again. His knuckles were white on the steering wheel, and his jaw was clenched. She should have made him wait outside the ultrasound room. Seeing the images of her baby for the first time was completely awe-inspiring. She could only imagine how they had shaken Nick.

But if he couldn't handle an ultrasound, how was he going to deal with an actual baby? She needed a strong partner.

A little niggle of guilt prodded her conscience. She'd known how apprehensive he was about this baby. She could have eased him into it a little more gently.

But why should she? The reality was they were having a baby, and it was time for him to either step up to the plate or walk away for good.

Nick slowed as he drove through the business district of Otter Tail, then pulled the sleek sports car into a parking spot at the curb.

He jumped out and opened her door, then helped her out. As soon as she was on the sidewalk, he dropped her hand as if it had burned him. "Do you, uh, want to get something to eat?"

"I have some leftovers in my refrigerator from Jen's restaurant. She sneaks up there and leaves them once in a while. Why don't I pack you some to take away with you?"

"Fine." He walked beside her, his hands jammed into his pockets, and didn't say anything. By the time they were in her apartment, the silence had become awkward.

She shed her sweater and purse, then pulled out the ultrasound picture and set it on the bookcase, next to a photo of her with her parents on their sailboat. The three of them stood together, laughing, arms draped over each other's shoulders. A unit. A family. As she stared at them side by side, the smiling figures blurred.

Her parents would never know their grandchild. Never hold her. Never teach her to sail, to play baseball, take her camping.

Sierra's mom had teased her about giving them grandchildren, warning they would spoil the kids unmercifully. "We won't have to worry about discipline," she'd joked. "We'll spoil them silly, then hand them back to you. I can't wait!"

Below the pictures sat a colorful box that held her mother's journals. Sierra touched it, needing to feel a connection to her parents. To something *they'd* touched.

"What's wrong?" Nick said behind her. He put his hands on her shoulders. "Why are you crying?"

"Missing my parents," she said, her voice catching. "Thank you for going with me to the ultrasound."

His hands tightened and his lips brushed her hair, his breath tickling her scalp. "You're welcome."

She turned and burrowed into his chest, the leather of his jacket cool against her hot cheek. His arms circled her slowly and awkwardly. His body hummed with tension, as if he was afraid to touch her.

She tried to ease away. "I'm sorry. That was…it was inappropriate," she said, her voice drowning in tears. "I won't do it again."

He cupped her head and tucked her against him, his fingers threading through her hair. "Don't," he said. "Let me hold you. I didn't want to cross a line." He swept his thumb over her cheek. "I don't know what you want from me."

"Just hold me," she whispered. She needed to feel his arms around her. Feel as if she was connected to another person, even if just for a few minutes. She'd been welcomed in Otter Tail, but wasn't close to anyone. No one had touched her, and she was aching for contact with another person.

Her breath shuddered in and out as she pressed against him. Keeping one hand around her, he pulled off his jacket with the other, then folded her against his chest. He dropped a kiss on her hair, and she shivered as his fingers moved gently against her nape.

When she realized she was brushing her lips to his sweater, she eased away, her face hot. "I didn't mean to cry all over you again. I'm sorry you've borne the brunt of my emotional meltdowns."

Instead of letting her go, he cupped her face in his palms. "This isn't a meltdown. Of course you're missing your parents. You're entitled to cry."

He pulled her close again, and the heat of his body, his arms around her, his scent, were comforting. She closed her eyes and allowed herself to relax into him. Maybe she was wrong about him. Nick thought he had nothing to give her. He'd told her he didn't do relationships, and maybe that was true. But he'd been remarkably sensitive to what she needed.

She was foolish to get her hopes up. Right now, though, he was giving her exactly what she needed.

CHAPTER ELEVEN

NICK LOOKED DOWN AT Sierra's dark red hair as she lifted her head and pushed away from him. Without thinking, he held her more closely. "Stay," he said quietly. "Let me hold you." Her tears of grief for her parents were painful to watch. He wasn't any good at comfort, but he could man up and give her this.

She glanced up, unsure, and he slid his hand over her silky hair and urged her against him. Her fists tightened on his sweater. "I didn't think you wanted any part of this."

"Define 'this'." He bent his head closer, then stopped. Waiting for her to answer.

Her nails grooved the thin material of his sweater and pressed against his skin. "This stuff—a pregnant woman's emotional roller coaster. Me falling apart. You having to comfort me."

"You're right. This isn't the way I'd choose to spend my afternoon. But you just lost your parents a few months ago. Who else is going to do it?"

"Most men run when women start to cry."

He was one of them. "Yeah, well, you haven't soaked my sweater yet. If you do, we'll rethink things."

She sniffled and smiled weakly. "You have hidden depths, Nick."

No, he didn't. He'd never made a secret of what he wanted or how he felt. "I like holding you, Sierra. I like touching you."

"Don't sell yourself short. You knew what I needed and gave it to me."

"Don't make me into someone I'm not," he said. He let her go and backed away. "I'm not one of those guys you usually date—understanding and sensitive and kind. I'm not a nice guy, Sierra."

She swiped at her eyes and studied him. "How do you know what kind of guys I date?"

He shoved his hands into his pockets. "I've seen them at the Christmas parties and the summer picnics." They hovered over her, waiting to do whatever she asked of them. Bland, eager-to-please puppies with wagging tails.

"I'm not the kind of woman you get involved with, either," she said.

So she'd noticed his dates, as well. There was no deep, inner meaning. It just proved they were both architects—they had an eye for detail and a good memory. "We're in unfamiliar territory, then." He moved one of the pictures of her family on the bookshelf, aligning it carefully with the others. "I guess we both have a lot to learn."

"I guess we do."

She was looking at him as if she'd figured something

out, and it made him uneasy. "You said something about food?" he said.

She smiled, and the softening of her expression, as if he'd said something much more profound than "let's eat," deepened his uneasiness.

"I did. Let's see what Jen left for me."

They walked into the bright, sunny kitchen. Nick could see a slice of the lake from the window over the sink, and the waves had picked up a little. If he opened the window, he'd be able to hear it. Sierra went to the refrigerator and peered inside. "There's chicken and mashed potatoes, and a thin-crust pizza." She smiled over her shoulder at him. "Jen doesn't appreciate Chicago-style pizza."

He moved closer and leaned over to look. "That's a wimpy-ass pizza." He set a hand on her shoulder to steady her. "Let's have the chicken."

"Good choice." She pulled it out. "You'll have to stay and eat because it's too hard to take away."

They put the chicken in the oven to warm it and set the potatoes in the microwave. He opened the refrigerator again. "How about a salad, too?" Pregnant women were supposed to eat healthy food. Salads were about as healthy as it got.

"That sounds good. You want to make it?"

"I can do that." As he cut up a tomato and cucumber, he glanced at Sierra, heating up the chicken. This was domestic, he thought uneasily. Cozy. As he watched her, his hand slipped and the knife sliced into his finger.

He should have known better than to try and do the

domestic thing. He shoved the cold water on and held his finger beneath the stream.

He was trying to be someone he wasn't.

"You cut yourself," Sierra said, dropping the plate of chicken on the counter.

"Just clumsy," he said lightly as he wrapped a piece of paper towel around his finger.

"I think I have some bandages."

"Don't worry about it. I'm fine."

She glanced at his hand more than once, but by the time they sat down to eat, he'd stopped bleeding. "Thanks for sacrificing your finger to help get things ready."

He paused with a bite of chicken halfway to his mouth. "Did you think I'd sit there and let you do all the work?"

"Of course not. But some guys would have."

"Losers, maybe."

She laughed. "This is why we've always worked so well together, Nick. We think the same way."

No, they didn't. He set his fork down and took a drink of water. They wanted completely different things from life.

Trying to change the subject, he asked her about the Barnes house and her plan of attack, now that they'd replaced the defective plywood flooring. After she described what she had planned for the coming week, he told her about the building he was working on. He asked her about a tricky design problem and they debated several solutions. Some of the tightness in his chest eased.

It was as if they were back at Boone and Associates, nothing more than colleagues.

Sierra lined up her fork and knife carefully on the empty plate, then moved her glass of water to one side. "One of the reasons I was upset earlier was because our baby won't have any grandparents. On my side, at least."

She drew circles in the condensation the glass had left on the wood table, and avoided his gaze. "How about you? Are your parents still alive?"

A vise clamped over his chest. "No. No parents."

She looked at him then. "Any other family? Sisters or brothers? Aunts? Uncles?"

"No family at all."

A tiny line appeared between her eyebrows. "But you know about them, right? For medical stuff? Like any diseases that run in the family?"

"No diseases I know about." Except an allergy to parenthood. That, they'd passed on to him.

The walls of a cage were closing in, and he edged away from the table. He wanted to step up to the plate for her. Intended to. But she was crowding him. Asking for more than he could give.

"Isn't there anything you can tell me about your family?"

"Stop pushing, Sierra," he said, more harshly than he'd intended. "I'm giving you what I can."

"That's not much, Nick." She'd stopped playing with her silverware and glass, and watched him steadily. "I know nothing about you, outside of work. And less about your family."

"What more do you want to know about me? We've worked together for three years. You should have a pretty good idea what I'm like."

"When two people are going to have a baby together, they generally know more about each other than their partner's opinions on window elevations." She watched him for a moment, then added, "You said you'd try to be part of our lives. That means we're part of your life, too."

We meant her and the baby. She thought that gave her the right to pry into his life. Into his soul. To pick at him until she'd uncovered all his secrets. "I said I'd be part of your life, and I intend to be." It was becoming clear that money was all he had to offer her. "My family is irrelevant. They're not around. I'm all there is."

"Okay." Her voice was quiet. Subdued. "Thank you for telling me."

He carried his dishes to the sink, rinsed them and put them in the dishwasher, then did the same with hers. "I need to get going," he said. "I have to get back to Chicago."

"I thought you were staying for the weekend."

"No. I have to go." He glanced around the kitchen, which had seemed so cozy and comfortable earlier. Now it was too small and confining. "I'll call you, all right?"

"Okay." She walked into the living room again.

He grabbed his jacket off the couch and threw it on. "So long, Sierra. I'll be in touch."

Without waiting for an answer, he opened the door and bolted down the stairs. As he slid into his car, he glanced up at her apartment. She stood at the window, watching him.

He held her gaze for a long moment, longing and regret and fear roiling inside him. Then he raised one hand to her, closed the car door and turned on the engine. Without looking back, he roared out of town.

SIX HOURS LATER, NICK was sitting in his attorney's office. Joe McCormick leaned back in his chair and frowned. "What's going on, Boone, that couldn't wait until Monday? I had to cancel dinner with a gorgeous brunette to meet with you."

"I need you to set up a trust fund, as well as a document giving up all custody rights. And I'll need a separate document outlining support payments."

His attorney shot upright. "Custody? Support? You have a kid?"

"Not yet. She's pregnant."

"You knocked up one of your babes?"

"She's not a *babe*," Nick said sharply. His hand tightened into a fist, but because Joe was one of his oldest friends, he forced himself to open his hand. Staring out the window at the skyscrapers surrounding the Loop building, he added, "And she's not mine, either."

"Tell me what's going on, Nick."

He used as few words as possible to sketch out the

situation. When he was finished, Joe said, "So let me get this straight. One of the women who works for you is pregnant after a one-night stand. You're going to dump a shitload of money onto her and the kid, sign away custody and never see her or the kid again."

"In a nutshell."

Joe tapped his pen on the table. "Did she ask for that much money? Did she tell you she didn't want you in the kid's life?"

"No." Nick stood up and paced to the window. "She thinks we can do the whole family thing—a cozy little unit with a mommy and daddy and happily ever after." God. The only thing he knew about being a parent was fear. Resentment. Hatred.

Loss.

"So this is all you. You don't want anything to do with her and the kid."

He *couldn't* have a kid. Any child of his would probably grow up as screwed up as he was. No, this baby would be far better off with Sierra and some nice, uncomplicated guy. A man who could give the kid what it needed. Who could give Sierra what she needed.

A man who believed there was such a thing as happily ever after.

Nick stared out the window, but all he saw was Sierra's expression when he'd said he had to leave. Pain. Regret. Sorrow. He remembered how she'd felt as she'd held on to him—the hard bump at her waist, the softness of the rest of her. The tears that had dripped onto his sweater.

He thought he'd escaped the cage she was weaving around him, but it had only followed him back to Chicago.

"Nick?"

He heard pity in his friend's voice, and clenched his teeth. "Just set up the trust and the rest of it. Send the documents to me when they're ready, and I'll have my accountant handle the money end of things." He took a deep breath. "I can't give her what she wants. This will have to do."

SIERRA HAD HAD TROUBLE focusing in the ten days since Nick left, but Mark's words pushed everything else from her mind. "Tell me I didn't hear you right, Mark."

"I wish I could," he said. "But it's true. There's a problem with the framing wood. It's at least two grades below what we ordered."

"I looked at those two-by-fours myself," she said, pushing away from the desk. "Every damn bundle of them. They were exactly what we ordered."

"Come take a look."

Her boots echoed on the plywood floors as she strode through the house. Mark's brother was working with the carpenters, and nodded at her as she walked by. "Hey, Sierra."

"How's it going, Kyle?" she said automatically as she scanned the studs that had already been nailed into place.

"Good. It's all good." He aimed his nail gun at a stud and pulled the trigger.

"This looks fine," she said to Mark.

"Look back here." He led her to the far corner of the house and pointed at a pile of two-by-fours on the floor. Mark pulled off the top studs, and the ones below were full of knots. Some were crooked. "This is crap wood," he said.

Sierra nudged a pile with her toe. The lengths beneath the top boards were just as bad. "What the hell is going on?"

"Kyle," Mark yelled. "Get over here."

The younger man set down his nail gun and hurried over. "What's up?"

"You supervised the delivery of this wood. It's not what we ordered."

Kyle frowned. "It looked fine to me."

"Did you undo any of the bundles and check inside?" He scowled at his brother. "Does this look like premium, kiln-dried wood?"

"The outside stuff was fine. Sorry, I should have opened them up." Kyle hurried back to work before Mark could say anything else.

"He's right, Mark," Sierra said, laying her hand on the contractor's sleeve. "I did the same thing. I looked at every bundle, and the outside pieces were all good. Someone deliberately hid the cheap stuff on the inside."

Mark kicked at the pile of wood and sent a few lengths spinning. "Yeah. That didn't happen accidentally."

"The plywood must have been deliberate, too," Sierra said. "Someone is substituting cheaper product and pocketing the difference." It happened at construction sites, but usually on bigger jobs, where it was easier to hide sub-spec material.

"Okay, we're going to get to the bottom of this. It's been wood both times, so it has to be one of the carpenters."

"We have to look at the lumberyard, too," Sierra pointed out. "The person putting together the order or loading it could be doing it."

"Vern claims none of his guys are involved."

"I'm guessing he's wrong," Sierra said flatly. "How long is this going to set us back?"

"Depends if any of this crap has been nailed into place yet."

"Let's find out." Sierra kicked aside a board in front of her and began checking every stud as the carpenters watched uneasily. Kyle and a couple of the others kept an eye on her and Mark, at the same time texting on their cell phones.

"Kyle! Jake! Chris! We're not paying you to play with your toys," Sierra called. "All of you, start checking every stud."

An hour later, they'd found that only a dozen inferior studs had been nailed into place. Sierra turned to the six carpenters. "I want to know who is responsible for this."

Silence. No one moved. No one looked at her, either.

"We'll get to the bottom of it," she warned. "And when

we do, the person who's been switching products will be arrested. If you want us to cut you any breaks, you can talk to me. I'll see what I can do for you."

Mark had disappeared into the trailer while she talked to the carpenters. As she was walking back, he emerged.

"Here are the specs for the wood. The purchase order clearly calls for the premium studs." He handed her the sheet as he held the door open for her.

She glanced at it, then crushed it in her fist. "Maybe we need to find a different lumberyard."

"Maybe we do." He grabbed her hand and removed the paper, but didn't let her go as he reread it. "I called Walker and told him there was a problem. They're coming over."

She yanked her hand away. "God, Mark, couldn't you have given me a little warning? An hour or two to pull it together?"

"You know that's not the way it works. The sooner we address this, the sooner we deal with it and move forward."

She sank into her chair, knowing he was right. She'd been off balance since the scene with Nick. They'd had a fight, he'd run away and clearly he'd made his choice. Eventually she'd get used to him not being part of their lives. She alternated between rage and grief, and her hormones had made her disgustingly weepy. Too emotional about everything.

She took a deep, shaky breath. This was her job. People in construction didn't do emotion. If there was a problem, you fixed it. You didn't sit around and whine about it.

"I'm sorry," she said. "You're right. I apologize." She moved to the window and looked at the piles of wood on the ground, the carpenters standing around. Not working. "This is my first solo project, and I screwed up." This was a major problem. Maybe big enough to make Walker believe she wasn't up to it.

Mark stepped behind her and touched her arm. Reading her mind, he said, "He's not going to fire you. You're doing fine—you're the most organized architect I've worked with. We'll figure this out."

His hand lingered a moment too long, and she knew it wasn't an accident. She'd noticed the expression on his face when she caught him watching her, and she knew he was interested. She wished she could be interested back.

Mark was a good man. He was funny, smart, and good at his job. And very easy on the eyes. But there was no spark for her. Not even a tiny one.

She wasn't sure why. He was the kind of guy any woman would want.

She turned to face him. "This isn't a good idea," she said gently. "I like you, Mark, but not that way." She forced a smile. "And I come with way too much baggage." She smoothed her shirt over her belly.

"I don't mind your baggage."

If she had to get pregnant, why couldn't it have been with someone like Mark? An uncomplicated, nice guy. Someone who'd make a great father.

"Sorry, Mark. It's not going to happen."

He stepped back, and she'd begun to edge away when the door to the trailer opened, bringing in warm, lake-scented air. Jen walked in, then froze. "Am I interrupting something?"

"Not at all," Sierra said, although her neck burned. "Mark and I were just discussing our problem."

"Really?" she murmured, her gaze snapping from Sierra to Mark. "I hope it's not serious."

"I'm afraid it might be." Flustered, Sierra smoothed the wrinkled purchase order and handed it to her. Walker followed his wife into the trailer and peered over her shoulder. With four people and all the desks, the work space was way too small.

"Someone is stealing from us," Sierra said. "The outside layer of two-by-fours was what the specs call for. The rest was much cheaper wood."

"How the hell did this happen?" Walker asked.

"It's either someone here, or someone at the lumber-yard," Sierra answered. "Maybe both, working together. We'll get to the bottom of it."

After they looked at the defective wood, Walker drew her away from the others. "How long is this going to delay the house? Jen is going nuts in that tiny place." He glanced over her shoulder. "She told me you know about…our news. She needs to have this house done so she has time to get everything ready." He glanced again at his wife and smiled. He didn't look like a hard-nosed businessman. He looked like a man deeply in love.

"I can give her anything she wants," he added. "I'd

give her the world, if she'd let me. But the only thing she asked for is a bigger house." He gazed at Sierra, and the businessman was back. "You need to make this happen. Figure out who's stealing from me and have them arrested."

"I will."

Walker was watching his wife again, and a tiny stab of jealousy pierced Sierra. She hoped someday a man would look at her the way Walker looked at Jen. As if she was everything to him.

"Fast," he added, jerking her attention back to him.

"As fast as I can."

He nodded. "I hope so."

As they said goodbye, Jen looked from Sierra to Mark again. "We'll talk to you soon," she said.

Sierra and Mark watched the SUV drive away, leaving a plume of dust in its wake. Then the contractor sighed. "He's got a reputation in the business world. He's tough. And when he wants something, he takes no prisoners."

"Then we better get busy."

TWO DAYS LATER, THEY hadn't made any progress. Everyone at the lumberyard had denied being involved. None of the carpenters came to her. They'd gotten new studs and the framing was continuing, but knowing that someone was sabotaging her project put Sierra on edge.

As she was ordering the plywood for the outside of the house, she heard the rumble of a large vehicle approaching. She leaned over to peer out the window, and her stomach clenched when she saw that it was Walker.

He was here to find out if they'd learned who was doing this. Sierra had expected him to give them another day or two, and she rifled through the papers on her messy desk to locate the list of things she'd already done. She found it just as Walker came through the door.

"Hi, Sierra. I've brought in someone to help you," he said. "This problem is setting back our finish date, and we need more eyes on the site. From now on, he's part of the team. I hope you can work together."

"I've never had a problem working with anyone," she said.

"Good. Let's not make this the first time."

A car door slammed outside, and Walker glanced over his shoulder. "Hope you didn't hurt your suspension on the ruts," he said to the person walking up the steps.

"I'm going to have to get an SUV," a familiar voice said, then Nick appeared in the doorway. "Hello, Sierra."

CHAPTER TWELVE

"Nick." Her heart banged against her sternum and her chest was too tight. The papers she held trembled, and she set them on the desk. "What are you doing here?"

His blue eyes were flat. Cold. "Barnes hired me to help you out. He said you were having a theft problem."

"Mark and I are handling it." She looked at Walker and struggled to maintain her composure as her anger threatened to boil over. She was a professional. She would act like one. "Walker, why didn't you ask for an update before hiring…someone else?" She hated the catch in her voice, hated that she was revealing her agitation. But she couldn't work with Nick. Couldn't spend hours with him in this tiny trailer. She'd accepted that he wasn't going to be part of her life, or her baby's, and now she just wanted to forget about him.

"You've had two incidents, and I don't want another one. We need more people keeping an eye on things. Jen suggested Nick, and I agreed." Walker's tone of voice said there would be no discussion. He'd already told her he would give his wife anything she asked for.

Why would Jen have suggested Nick? And why had he agreed? He didn't have time to take on this job. Sierra's hand tightened on the papers. "Mark and I will make sure nothing else happens."

Walker shrugged. "With Boone here, we'll be more sure, won't we?"

She focused on Walker, rather than her anger. "I'm going to personally inspect every piece of material that comes onto this job site. You don't have to spend money on another architect." She swallowed once, then again. Coldness had crept into her voice, and she couldn't allow that. Couldn't let Walker see how upset she was.

"Money isn't a problem," Walker said. "I'm sorry if I've insulted you, Sierra. But bottom line, I don't really care. This is the deal. Take it or leave it."

Either she accepted Nick and agreed to work with him, or Walker would fire her. She stared blindly at her messy desk. "I'll think about it."

"Let me know what you decide," he said. He walked out of the trailer and closed the door behind him.

Silence echoed in the too-warm room. The only sound was the relentless pounding of waves. There had been a storm last night, and the lake was still restless.

Nick hadn't moved any closer. He stayed by the door, watching her. She didn't look at him, but felt his gaze sliding over her, as intimate as a touch.

She took a deep breath and forced herself to face him. "Why did you do this? Why did you take the job? You knew you'd have to work with me."

He pushed away from the door and walked over to

examine their bulletin board. "Barnes didn't give me a choice."

"That's ridiculous."

He was standing with his hands in the pockets of his jeans. His back was rigid, his shoulders tense. He looked as if he wanted to hit something.

"What could he possibly hold over your head?" Sierra asked.

He spun around. His teeth were clenched and a muscle jumped in his jaw. "You, Sierra. He threatened me with you. If I didn't agree to this, he said he'd fire you. Since you seem so set on the happy little family idea, I assumed you'd figured out a way to get me up here."

It took a moment for his words to sink in. Then another hot wave of anger swept over her. "You think I *asked* him to do this? That I *wanted* you here?"

"Why else would he do it? You don't need me on this job, and I told him so. You're perfectly capable of solving any problem that comes up. He didn't pay any attention—he'd already made up his mind."

"Not because of me," she said, hearing her voice rise and not caring. "You're the last person I would have asked him to hire. After that weekend, do you really think I want you around?"

"Of course I do. What else was I supposed to think? You want me involved with the kid. You grilled me about my family. You wanted to analyze my feelings. I could feel the walls closing in."

She'd tried to go beyond the superficial, and he'd

freaked out. He didn't want any kind of intimacy with her. Sadness for herself, for Nick, for her child churned with anger at his assumptions.

"Nick, *you* insisted on coming to the ultrasound. *You're* the one who wanted to stick around."

"Because that's what you wanted."

"No, it's not. I *told* you I don't want my baby to have a resentful father. I only wanted you around if that was your choice. When you left so suddenly and didn't call, it wasn't hard to figure out that you'd made your decision." She took a deep breath and tried to steady herself. "And that was okay. I don't want someone unreliable in my life. I'm glad I found out now that I can't count on you." She would be, anyway, as soon as she stopped being so hormonal and stupidly emotional. "I wanted to forget about you, Nick. So why would I ask Walker to bring you back?"

It looked as if Nick flinched. He watched her pace, and when she got close to him, he stepped in front of her.

"You mean that."

His eyes had thawed, and now looked puzzled. She clenched her fists to keep from shoving him through the door and out of her life. "Of course I mean it. Why would you think I didn't?"

"When Walker called, I assumed you'd put him up to it."

"You thought I was playing some kind of game? Have I ever been less than straight with you? Have I ever tried to go behind your back? If I wanted to get in touch with you, Nick, I would have." She sucked in a breath and tried to steady her breathing. "Now that I know you're not interested in us, I don't want to see you again."

"You said you wanted me to get involved."

He appeared uncertain, and she ignored the sympathy trying to gain a foothold. She didn't want to feel sorry for Nick.

She threw open the door, and the wind caught it and pinned it against the side of the trailer. "You chose not to when you walked away, told me you would call, and didn't. Now get out of *my* trailer and take yourself back to Chicago."

"I can't do that."

"Sure you can. You just slide into that little toy of yours—" she jerked her head in the direction of his sports car "—and turn it around. I'll bet you have a navigation system in that baby that will take you straight home."

Without removing his eyes from her, he pulled the door closed. "If I leave, he's going to fire you."

"Why would you care? It doesn't affect your bottom line. You're not getting paid for this project."

He did flinch at that. "You're pregnant with…" He stopped, then continued, "I couldn't let him do that."

Nick couldn't even say that she was pregnant with *his* baby. "Not your problem, Nick. *I'm* not your problem. Or your responsibility."

She sat down at her desk and centered the stack of papers on her calendar. The sentences and words on the top sheet blurred together, but she pretended she was reading them. She picked up a pencil and a legal pad and scribbled some notes. Turned the sheet over and read the next one.

He pulled the stack out of her hands. "We need to talk."

She snatched it back. "I'm done talking."

He dropped into the chair across the desk from her. "I didn't set this up. If you didn't, either, who did?"

Instead of throwing something at his head, she took a deep breath. Tried to clear the buzz of anger from her brain. Rage and emotion would get her nowhere. Walker had created a dilemma for them, and Nick was right. They had to think this through. "Walker. And Jen. He said it was what she wanted."

"Jen wanted him to hire me?"

"She's in a hurry to get into a new house." It was none of his business why.

"There are a hundred other architects they could hire, a lot of them closer than Chicago. So why me?"

"How would I know? I barely know Jen." But Sierra's brain nudged her with the memory of the way Jen had watched her and Nick at the house, and then again at the Harp that night. How Jen had walked in on her and Mark when he was standing too close. A horrible suspicion arose. "I'll talk to her, though. I'll find out."

"I'll go with you."

The hell he would. She wasn't going to question Jen about her motives in front of Nick. "No. I'll do it myself. You can head back to Chicago."

"What are you going to do after they fire you?"

"As I said, not your concern." Sierra was proud of how cool she sounded. She opened a file drawer and pulled out a folder at random. "Be careful when you leave. The ruts are deeper than they look. You don't want to get stuck."

She put her head down and pretended to study the top paper in the folder. Nick didn't move. Finally, he said, "As long as I'm here, why don't you fill me in on what's been going on?"

She raised her eyebrows. "No, thanks. As you pointed out, I'm perfectly capable of dealing with the problem." Back when she worked for him, she would have gone to him immediately. They'd brainstorm together and come up with a creative solution to problems.

She missed that. They had gotten to the point where they used a kind of shorthand when working out a problem. Sometimes, she'd thought they could look at a drawing or a design idea and know what the other was thinking before saying a word.

Occasionally, on this project, she'd felt as if she was thrashing around in a vacuum. That was only because she was working alone. It was a different process and she was still getting used to it. Eventually she'd be fine.

"I know you're capable." He scowled. "That's what I told Barnes. But I drove a hell of a long way to get here. Give Barnes his money's worth for today, at least."

"Walker gets his money's worth every day," she said coolly. She worked damn hard on this house. "Since we had the second incident, I'm here before anyone else and I'm the last person to leave."

"You're here by yourself?" he asked sharply.

"Again, none of your business." When she saw actual concern in his expression, she sighed. "I'm not stupid. Mark has been here, too."

"Good. That's good," Nick muttered. He glanced out the window and stilled. After a moment, she saw Mark walking toward the trailer. "Get rid of him. We're not done here."

"You're no longer my boss and I won't take orders from you." She gathered the papers she needed to work on tonight. She'd work from home, where she could lock herself in her apartment and not have to think about Nick.

"Goodbye, Nick." She held open the door. He stared at her for a moment, as if debating whether or not to leave. Then Mark started up the stairs, and Nick brushed past both of them, hurried to his car and climbed in.

"What was that about?" Mark asked as they both watched him drive away.

"Walker got a bug in his ear that I needed help. I'm going to straighten him out."

"Your old boss is interested in you." Mark looked away from the rooster tail of dust trailing Nick's car. "Is it mutual? Is that why you brushed me off?"

She'd taken enough crap from the men in her life this afternoon. She wasn't going to deal with this, too. "I'm not interested in Nick Boone. I brushed you off because there's no chemistry." She softened her voice.

"I'm trying to be professional here, Mark. I like you and I like working with you. Okay?"

As if he hadn't heard a word she said, Mark nodded at her abdomen. "He have anything to do with that?"

Her hand clenched the papers she held, so hard they crumpled along one edge. "Leave, Mark. Now."

He opened his mouth, and she raised her hand. "Don't. Not a word. Just go."

He hesitated for a long moment, then nodded once, spun on his heel and hurried down the stairs.

She stood at the door until his pickup disappeared, then closed the door and sank into her chair. She swiveled to face the bulletin board, which was covered with reports, letters, contracts, estimates and schedules. Two months of work, hundreds of hours of labor. A labor of love.

She swung around and stared blindly out the window. The house was still all bones, just plywood flooring and partially finished frame. But it would be lovely when it was done. She'd designed Jen and Walker's house to take maximum advantage of this view. Birch and maple trees, fully leafed out, framed the small strip of beach. Jumbled rocks formed a natural barrier at each end and would keep trespassers away. The lake was gray today, with whitecaps rolling a hundred yards from shore. When it calmed, it would be a deep blue-green. If she stepped outside, she'd hear birds singing and leaves rustling in the wind.

She knew this piece of land. Knew what Jen and Walker wanted. She saw their vision, and her design had reflected it. The theft was a problem, but it wasn't going to delay them for more than another day or so.

She and Mark would figure out who was responsible. They just had to do more digging.

This house was going to be the perfect blend of form and function. She ached to work on it. Yearned to finish the job, to look at it when it was done and know that she had brought it to life.

On top of that, it would be an impressive addition to her portfolio. It would show prospective clients what she was capable of. It would ease the way for more commissions.

And she could have all that, but only if she agreed to work with Nick for the next few months. If she agreed, essentially, to let him supervise her.

She stared out the window for a long time, until the shadows of the trees reached across the sandy soil and covered the trailer. Finally, knowing what she had to do, she stood up, stuffed the papers she needed into her briefcase, and walked out of the trailer.

CHAPTER THIRTEEN

SHE WAS PRETTY CERTAIN Jen would be here. On a busy Wednesday night at the supper hour where else would she be but her restaurant?

When Sierra walked in, a group of six was waiting to be seated and an attractive, dark-haired woman stood at the podium. She smiled at Sierra. "Hi, and welcome. How many in your party?"

"I'm not here to eat," Sierra said. "I need to talk to Jen."

The woman's smile was unwavering. "She isn't available right now. May I help you?"

Sierra had eaten here several times already and thought she'd recognize all the hostesses. "I'm sorry, but who are you?"

The woman stepped from behind the podium. She wore a dark suit and a white silk shirt and looked very professional. Few of the people who ate at The Summer House dressed this well. "I'm Kerry Clare-Piantek, her new assistant. And you are…?"

"I'm Sierra Clark. Her architect. There's a problem with the house I'm building for her, and I need to see her."

"I'll be happy to give her a message."

"Never mind. I need to see her myself."

Sierra stepped away from the podium, dodged the woman and headed for the kitchen. Kerry followed, saying, "She hired me to handle problems for her. I can't let you go back there."

"Are you going to tackle me and take me down in front of everyone? Because that's the only way you're going to stop me. Of course, that would give you a problem to handle."

A ripple of laughter swept the room as Sierra pushed through the swinging doors into the kitchen. A quick glance told her that Jen wasn't on the floor, so she headed for the office.

The door was closed, but Sierra shoved it open. Kerry was right on her heels. Jen looked up and stilled when she saw them.

"I tried to stop her, Jen," Kerry said. "She didn't pay any attention."

"No," Jen answered, watching Sierra. "I'm sure she didn't." She transferred her gaze to her assistant. "It's okay, Kerry. Close the door behind you, please."

Sierra waited to hear the click, then said, "I quit. I'll clean my stuff out of the trailer tomorrow, and I'll be out of the apartment the next day. If you're interested in the plans for the house, I'm willing to discuss selling them to you."

She turned to leave, and heard Jen's chair scrape against the floor. "Sierra, wait."

Sierra opened the door, but Jen pushed past her to

nudge it closed. "Wait a damn minute. You can't march in here and say you're quitting, then leave without an explanation."

Sierra whirled to face her. "Do you really need an explanation? You're a smart woman, Jen. Why do you think I'm quitting?"

Jen was still wearing her chef's whites, and she sank onto the edge of her desk. Guilt flickered across her face. "Nick showed up today."

"See, I knew you could figure it out." She turned to leave.

"Wait, Sierra." Jen put a hand on her arm, and she shook it off. "Please. I don't want you to quit."

Sierra swung around to face her. "Then why did you do such a dumb-ass thing?"

"I thought you two were... I thought you'd be happy to see him."

"No. I was not happy to see him. And I'm not working with him."

"Is he the father of your baby?"

Sierra sucked in a breath as humiliation washed over her. Had she been that obvious? Had everyone else seen it, too? "That's not relevant."

The sound of a dish splintering on the floor, followed by shouts in a foreign language, came from the kitchen. Metal clashed, as if someone had thrown a pan onto the stove. More yelling.

She didn't understand the language, but she had no trouble comprehending the message in the blur of sounds from the other side of the door.

Anger. Turmoil. Chaos.

Just like her life.

"You're really angry," Jen said slowly. "You're not just trying to make a point."

"Of course I am. Wouldn't you be? You told me Walker didn't want you to work while you're pregnant. What if he hired another chef, and said you could only keep cooking if you agreed to have him here? And oh, by the way, he's in charge. What would you do?"

"Walker wouldn't do that. He knows he doesn't have that right."

"You have the right to hire any damn architect you please to work on your house. Just like I can quit. But being my employer doesn't give you the right to manipulate me and Nick."

"I miscalculated," Jen said.

"Really." She held Jen's gaze while fury pumped through her. Part of her realized Jen was only trying to help. But the rest of her was enraged.

"I think Nick is your baby's father. I thought you wanted him around. I thought this was the perfect way to get the two of you together so you could work things out."

Sierra closed her eyes as Jen's words pierced her like an arrow. "There's nothing to work out. I don't want him around, and he doesn't want to be here. But you're welcome to hire him in my place."

She opened the door, but before she could step into the noisy kitchen, Jen said, "I'm sorry, Sierra. I'd tell him to go, but we've signed a contract with him. I want you to stay. Will you at least sleep on it?"

"Yes. But my answer isn't going to change tomorrow." Her throat swelled. "Goodbye, Jen."

NICK EASED OUT OF HIS CAR and glanced at the windows of the apartment above Jen's restaurant. The blinds were closed, but light leaked out around the edges and at the bottom. Sierra was probably home.

He'd just gotten off the phone with Walker, who'd told him Sierra had quit. Barnes had tried to apologize, but Nick had brushed him off. Now he had to figure out a way to fix this.

He crossed the street, squeezed into the tiny vestibule and rang Sierra's doorbell. He listened for movement above him, but didn't hear a thing. He was just about to leave when the door at the top of the stairs opened and Sierra looked down at him.

She wore a pair of gray sweatpants and a green sweatshirt with the sleeves pushed up, and her hair was pulled into a ponytail. The combination made her look impossibly young and defenseless.

Her clothes were so loose that her rounded belly was hidden. For a moment, it looked as if she wasn't pregnant, as if it had all been a horrible dream.

Then she reached into her apartment, and in silhouette, the curve of her abdomen was clearly visible. He thought she was going to disappear inside and ignore him, but instead the door buzzed to unlock.

She waited at the top of the stairs, blocking the

entrance to her home. He stopped two steps below her. "May I come in?"

She studied him for a moment, as if trying to decide, then vanished inside. He followed her and closed the door behind him.

There was a bucket with water and a sponge sitting on the floor near the blinds, and an assortment of cleaning supplies in another bucket close by. "What are you doing?" he asked.

"I'm cleaning the apartment before I leave," she said, sinking into the chair. Not the couch, which would have allowed him to sit next to her.

"You're not really quitting, are you?"

Her gaze was steady on him. "Did Jen call you? Did she expect you to sweet-talk me out of it?"

"Sweet-talk you?" He shifted on the couch, feeling uncomfortable. "Trust me, Sierra. If there's anyone who can do that, which I doubt, I know it's not me. I called Walker to chew him out, and he told me this whole thing was his wife's idea. I could hear him yelling at her, and she was yelling back." It had made him uncomfortable to witness their fight.

"Jen and Walker? Fighting?" She frowned. "You must be exaggerating. They're crazy about one another."

"Doesn't mean they can't fight." Janet got loud when she was upset, and Nick had heard her side of a few fights with Frank. They were the happiest couple he knew.

"Makes it unlikely," Sierra retorted. "But if Jen doesn't expect you to talk me into staying, what are you doing here?" She gave him a quizzical look, and shame scalded him.

She was genuinely surprised he'd come. Surprised he cared enough to try and fix things.

Of course she was. The last time she'd seen him, he'd torn out of Otter Tail as if the devil were after him. He'd made it plain he wasn't interested in what she wanted. This morning, he'd accused her of trying to force him to come back to town.

She hadn't expected anything from him. And why would she? He hadn't given her any indication that he wanted to help her.

He'd assumed she was playing games, like most of the women he dated. She wasn't. She was nothing like those women. She had quit her job, even though she was pregnant, without having another one lined up. It told him exactly how serious she was about wanting nothing to do with him.

"I underestimated you," he said quietly.

"Other than at work, I doubt you've ever really listened to a woman in your life." She levered herself out of the chair and bent to pick up the sponge from the bucket. She squeezed soapy water out of it, then began washing the top of the radiator. "You can see yourself out. I want to finish this tonight."

Because he was watching her so closely, he noticed how slowly her arm was moving. How long it took for her to stand up, then bend over again. She was exhausted, but she was still doing what she needed to do. Cleaning the apartment before she moved out, even though Jen and Walker could easily afford to pay someone to do it.

His respect for Sierra took another giant leap. "Would you sit down for a moment? Please?" he added.

She wiped off her hands with a towel from the floor, then turned to face him. "I'm not interested in anything you have to say."

"I know." She'd tried to tell him that more than once, and he finally got it. She was serious. She fully expected to raise this baby on her own. And he suspected that the money his attorney would soon begin to send her would go right into a savings account for the child. She wouldn't spend a cent of it on herself.

He'd never really *looked* at Sierra. He'd just lumped her in with all the women in his life. He'd never seen her as an individual. As a real person.

That was going to change, he vowed. Starting now. "Please don't quit your job. I want to try and make this work. Not just the job, but you and me. And the baby."

Nothing in her expression softened. Not even a glimmer appeared, showing she might be receptive. "I'm not a fool, Nick. Can you come up with one reason why I should buy that?"

"No, I guess I can't. Just my word."

Her jaw tightened. "How much do you think that's worth?"

He'd always prided himself on being a man of his word. Of keeping his promises, making good on his responsibilities. He hadn't done any of that with Sierra.

"Right now, nothing," he said. In his dealings with her, he'd betrayed everything he thought he stood for. "But that's going to change."

"You were humoring me the last time you said that. You had no intention of trying."

"You're right, and it was wrong of me. I'm sorry. I promise I'm not trying to humor you now."

She studied him as if he were a new species of insect. "I can't think why you'd imagine I'd believe you."

"I deserve everything you're saying. I get that. I have no way to convince you I'm sincere, and no credibility with you. All I'm asking for is a chance."

His leg began to twitch as he waited and watched her. She sank into the chair and pulled up her knees, then laid her head down on them. He read weariness in every line of her body. Who could she count on? Who would ease some of her burden?

That was supposed to be his job, as the father of her baby. Shame washed over him again. He'd been selfish. Self-centered. Unfeeling.

Not the traits of an honorable man. He'd done nothing right with Sierra.

He would fix that.

She looked so vulnerable in the chair. Fragile, as if a strong wind would blow her away. He wanted to hold her like he had after they'd returned from the ultrasound. Comfort her. Make her realize she wasn't alone.

He didn't have that right. One move in her direction, and she'd send him out the door.

Finally, she lifted her head. "You're going to have

to prove it this time. I'm a fool for giving you even that much, but I'll do it for my baby."

Her baby. She still wouldn't acknowledge that it was his baby, too.

Why would she? he reminded himself brutally. He'd told her and told her he wanted no part of it. Didn't want to be a father. Had no interest in becoming a family.

The whole idea still terrified him. Too many things could happen when you got attached to someone. Things that might destroy you.

But if Sierra could be this strong, he could, too. He would man up and do the right thing. Her independence, her strength, her determination made him feel small. They opened his eyes and made him actually see her.

He liked the person he saw.

"I'll do whatever it takes. Whatever you want."

"I'll give you a week to convince me," she said, as if she hadn't heard him. "Not a day more."

"Fine. I can accept that." He stood and held out his hand. "Let me help you put these cleaning supplies away."

She got up from the chair by herself, and he dropped his arm. He was going to have to earn every tiny sliver of trust. Without saying anything else, he gathered the rags and sponges and towels, picked up the two buckets and carried them into the kitchen. There was a tiny room behind it that led to a back door, and it held a laundry tub and stacked washer and dryer.

He dumped the dirty water and draped the rags over the edge of the tub, then turned to find her watching him. "You look tired," he said. "Have you eaten anything?"

"I'm fine." She leaned against the wall, and he suspected she needed the support. "You have to leave, Nick."

Instead of walking out the door, he washed his hands and opened the refrigerator. He spotted some leftover pizza, put it in the toaster oven to heat up, then slid it onto a plate and set it on the table. "Eat, Sierra."

She stood in the same place, watching him, and he couldn't read her expression. He used to have no trouble doing that. Every emotion she felt was reflected on her face.

Not anymore.

He was part of the reason she'd changed.

He didn't blame her for mistrusting him. After the miserable excuses for parents he'd had, he wasn't father material. He had nothing to give a child. But he was determined to try to help her.

He couldn't give her what she wanted. But he'd give her what he could, and hope it would be enough.

CHAPTER FOURTEEN

THE SUN WAS JUST RISING over Lake Michigan when Sierra unlocked the construction trailer the next morning. Smears of pink and orange streaked the sky, and a sliver of yellow edged the horizon. She set her cup of tea and container of yogurt, fruit and granola on the desk, then sank into her chair.

She was insane. She should be gathering her belongings from the trailer, tying up loose ends, then driving away from Otter Tail. Instead, she'd agreed to work with Nick for a week. Longer, if he did what he'd promised.

She tried to ignore the hope that had crept to life last night. If she took him at his word—again—and convinced herself that he was really willing to see where this went, she was doomed to disappointment. She would try to keep an open mind, try to give him the benefit of the doubt, but he was going to have to prove he was sincere. She didn't think he'd lied to her last night. At the time, he'd meant what he said. The question was whether he would mean it in the long run. Or even if he *could* mean it.

She suspected not.

But she'd give him the week. He was the baby's father, after all. When her child asked about him, years from now, Sierra wanted to be certain she'd done everything possible to keep Nick in his child's life.

She could risk seven days to do that.

Now she had to figure out how to get through it. How to guard her heart and her emotions, so that she didn't begin to count on him. How to keep the hope under wraps and under control.

She would be cool and professional and detached. They were working together, after all. She'd worked with him for almost three years and hadn't had a problem keeping her distance.

Except for that night.

Her hand shook as she set her tea on the desk, and a little splashed out and burned her hand.

She was sucking on the space between her thumb and index finger when the trailer door opened. She swiveled in her chair, and Nick walked in the door.

She let her hand drop when she realized he was looking at it. "Nick. I didn't hear your car."

"Not even my swearing as I hit those ruts?"

"Not that, either." He was dressed in jeans and a sweater over a button-down shirt, and he carried a briefcase. When she realized she'd been looking too long, she swiveled again and stared blindly at her computer screen.

"You're here early," she said, knowing it was the lamest phrase in the world.

"We have a lot of work to do." He glanced around the

trailer, assessing it. Cataloging everything. She knew how Nick approached a job. "Which desk can I use?"

"Mark's using that one." She gestured at the desk facing hers. "Any of the others are fine."

Nick stared at Mark's desk for a moment, as if considering taking it anyway, then swung his briefcase onto the one next to hers. She rubbed at the red skin between her thumb and index finger and cleared her throat.

"I've gotten everyone's schedule from Vern at the lumberyard. I'm going to eliminate people who weren't working both times we had problems. That should narrow it down for us."

"Right to business," he murmured.

"You just said we have a lot of work to do. Walker needs us to stay on schedule." Did he think she was going to get all emotional on the job? Bring their personal life into the office? She shifted so she was facing him. "Unless you want to discuss feelings. We can do that instead, if you like."

He stared at her for a long moment, and she thought his mouth twitched. "Work is good," he finally said. "Why didn't I see this side of you at B and A?"

"Which side would that be?" She bent over her computer again, pretending to be working.

"The snarky sarcasm."

"I save that for special people." She typed a sentence of complete gibberish.

"Good to know I'm special."

"Yeah, special like a mosquito bite." She felt his gaze on her as she typed more meaningless words. Finally, he opened his own computer. As he booted it up, she scribbled the Wi-Fi network password on a piece of paper and handed it to him.

"Password?"

"Yes."

"Thanks."

She told herself to ignore what he was doing, but noticed he followed the same routine she did first thing in the morning—check his email, check his Facebook account. When she found herself studying his dark hair and wondering why it was longer than usual, she turned to stare out the window. The sun had risen, and the sky was bright blue. Mark would be here soon. *Focus.*

"I've been researching theft at construction sites," she finally said. "It sounds as if there are usually at least two people involved—one at the supplier and another at the site."

"I've had a few situations like this. I'm sure it's why Walker wanted me here."

No, Jen wanted to play matchmaker.

But Sierra would use his expertise to solve her problem. "How did you finally figure out who it was?"

"I started with schedules, just like you're doing. When I narrowed it down, I confronted the people I suspected on the site. Once they broke down and confessed, they were happy to rat out their buddy at the supplier."

"I've always wanted to play good cop-bad cop," she said. "I'll be the bad cop."

Nick held her gaze. "That works. You intimidate the hell out of me."

She swung around to stare blindly at her computer screen. He thought she was intimidating?

Mark walked into the trailer just as Nick leaned toward her. Pushing away from her desk, she turned and smiled at the contractor, but he'd stopped in the doorway.

She'd tried to ignore her and Nick's personal problems and focus on the job, but Mark's hard stare brought everything back. She edged her chair away from Nick's, aware that he was watching her, too.

"Hey, Mark," she said, pleased when she sounded completely normal.

He pulled the door closed with a loud snap. "Good morning, Sierra." His pause lasted only a fraction of a second, but she noticed it. "Boone. I didn't think you were coming back."

"Three heads are better than two," he answered easily. "I was just telling Sierra that I've dealt with this kind of thing before."

"I have, too. And I know everyone involved."

"Good," Nick answered. "That'll make it easier to figure things out."

Mark stared at him, and Sierra had no trouble reading his expression—*we don't need you, hotshot.*

Mark didn't say anything for a moment. Then he nodded. "Great. Sierra, have you checked on the shingles?"

"I talked to the supplier a couple weeks ago, but one

of us should give them another call to make sure they're on schedule."

"I can do that," Mark said.

The three of them worked silently, occasionally scribbling something on a legal pad. Mark stared at her for a long time, trying to catch her attention, but she kept her gaze on her computer. Out of the corner of her eye, she saw Nick look from her to Mark, then back at her. Testosterone swirled in the air, ratcheting up the tension, making it hard to breathe. Finally, Mark stood up.

"Sierra, I need you to take a look at something outside."

As she rose, Nick did, too. "If it's work related, I'll come along."

Mark shook his head. "We can handle it, Boone."

Nick remained standing and the two men stared at each other. Sierra yanked open the door. "I'll meet you outside, Mark. I don't want to be in here when the pissing contest starts."

She let the door slam behind her, and Mark followed her out almost immediately. She could hear him hurrying to catch up.

"Wait, Sierra."

She whirled on him. "What, exactly, was all that about? You and Nick are acting like idiots."

Mark ran his fingers through his hair. "I know you don't want him here. I guess I'm upset for you."

Her irritation faded. "That's sweet of you, Mark, and yes, it was awkward when he showed up. But Nick and I have worked together for a long time, and he's right.

The three of us working together will figure this out more quickly."

"Yeah. I know." He sighed. "A month ago, I was thrilled I'd be working with Nick Boone. Now I just want him to leave." He gave her a level look. "I don't like the competition."

"Competition? For what?"

He continued to watch her, and she felt the heat rise in her neck. "Mark, there's no competition. I told you, I like you a lot—you're a great guy. But I'm not looking for anyone right now." She tucked a strand of hair behind her ear. "Any woman I know would be falling over herself to date you. I'm just not... I can't..." She sighed and put her hand on his arm. "I'm sorry."

"Nothing to apologize for," he said. He tried to smile. "I'm disappointed, but I'll probably live."

She stretched up and kissed his cheek. "If you get any nicer, I'm going to be dragging all my girlfriends here to meet you."

"Thanks, but I'll pass on that." He kicked a clod of sand-caked clay toward the lake. "I'm going to take another look at that wood."

He whirled and headed toward the deserted skeleton of the house. She watched him for a moment, then turned and headed for the trailer. It was barely eight o'clock, and she was already tired. It was going to be a long day.

AS THE DOOR CLOSED BEHIND Sierra and Mark, Nick sank into his chair to avoid the temptation to watch them out the window. It was none of his business if the two of them had something going on. But the thought burned a hole in his gut.

Hell, this was what he'd wanted—a nice guy who would make Sierra happy. Someone who would be a good father to her baby. *His baby, too,* a tiny voice whispered, but he ignored it.

Cameron qualified on all counts. And judging by the way the guy looked at Sierra, he was more than willing to take on the job.

Nick gave in and glanced out the window. They were standing too damn close together, and the conversation looked intense. Then Sierra put her hand on his arm and kissed his cheek.

Nick kicked the trash can hard enough to dent it, then shoved his hands into his pockets as he stared blindly at Sierra's bulletin board.

He had no rights with her. He'd gone out of his way to make it clear he wanted nothing to do with her. But even after he'd fled to Chicago and sworn he'd have no further contact with her, he'd woken from dreams of her almost every night.

Sierra had asked nothing from him. More, she'd made it abundantly clear she wanted no part of him or his money. She'd had the strength of will to quit her job rather than be forced into contact with him. And she was fiercely protective of that baby already.

He wondered if his mother had ever felt that way about him when she was pregnant.

She hadn't given him much thought once he was born.

And he'd judged every woman he'd dated against his mom. Expected the worst from all of them, and rarely been disappointed.

Sierra was completely out of his experience. The more he found out about her, the more she intrigued him.

The door opened, and Sierra tossed her jacket at the coat stand and threw herself into her seat. She rubbed her belly absently as she stared at the computer screen, ignoring him completely.

"Sierra," he began, and she whirled on him, her eyes narrowed.

"What, Nick? Do you have something to say?"

"About what?" he asked cautiously.

"About all that staring and chest thumping between you and Mark."

"What?" He couldn't take his eyes off her. Anger had brought color to her cheeks and her eyes sparked. She was breathing heavily, and he couldn't help staring at her chest. Were her breasts bigger?

"Eyes up here, Boone," she said.

He felt himself flush. "Sorry. What were you asking?"

"I want to know what all that pawing the ground and marking your territory was about."

He held up his hands. "The guy was hovering. It wasn't appropriate for a workplace, and I wanted him to know it. But if you want Cameron, that's fine with me. I'll mind my own business."

She rolled her eyes. "A huge part of the Y chromosome must be devoted to the genes for idiocy."

She whirled and faced her computer again, manipulating her mouse with jerky movements. Her face was still flushed and her shoulders tense.

"Do you?" He couldn't stop himself from asking. "Want Cameron?"

"Shut up and do some work," she answered, staring at her screen.

"He wants you, you know. He's a nice guy." Nick had to force the words from his clenched teeth.

She made a noise that sounded suspiciously like a snort. "Yeah, he's a great guy. But he *wants* me? I don't think so. I'm five months pregnant."

Nick couldn't stop himself from leaning closer. Her curves were ripe and lush. Her skin glowed and her hair caught the light and reflected it back. "Pregnancy agrees with you. Any man who looks at you would want you."

She started to answer, then her gaze caught his and held. Her eyes darkened to the color of whiskey, and her neck and cheeks turned pink. Her mouth opened a tiny bit and her breath caught.

"Not like this," she said. But she didn't look away.

"Exactly like this." He slowly moved his chair closer, watching, waiting for her to object. When she didn't tell him to stop, he put his hand over her belly. It was firm beneath his fingers, and warm. "You're beautiful."

For the first time, he felt a connection to that bump

beneath her shirt. He'd put that baby there. It had been conceived in grief and anguish, not love, but it was his.

She could have been his, too, if he hadn't been such an ass.

He wished he could rewind the tape and go back to the night she'd told him she was pregnant. He would handle it very differently. He wouldn't shove a check at her. Wouldn't tell her he wanted nothing to do with a baby.

He wasn't a good candidate for father of the year. Not for happily ever after, either. But he'd try, damn it.

"Nick?" Her voice was tentative. Unsure. But she didn't push him away. Her hand hovered over his, then dropped.

"Do you want him, Sierra?" he asked.

"Who?"

"Cameron."

"That's none of your business." But she didn't look away. In the heavy silence, Nick could hear her ragged breathing. Her lips were flushed red, her eyes huge.

"Do you know what I think?" He reached for her chair and pulled it toward him. The wheels creaked on the floor, then her knees bumped his.

She shoved him away as if the touch had burned her skin. She faced her computer, her hands on the keyboard, her chest rising and falling. "I don't want to know what you're thinking," she said, her voice hoarse. "I'm damn sure it would make me angry, and I have work to do."

He watched her pretend to work. For a moment,

before she caught herself, she'd wanted him, too. But before he could pursue it, he heard footsteps on the stairs.

Cameron. Nick swung his chair around and faced his computer. By the time the guy opened the door, both he and Sierra were pretending to work.

But all he could think about was that moment when Sierra had let down her guard.

Maybe, if Sierra was on his side, he could learn how to be a father.

CHAPTER FIFTEEN

SIERRA STARED AT HER computer screen, her heart thudding so hard she was sure both men could hear it. Nick had been about to kiss her.

She'd been about to kiss him back.

What was wrong with her? What had she been thinking?

She *hadn't* been thinking. She'd been feeling. The pregnancy hormones must be affecting her libido, because she'd almost leaned forward to press her mouth to his.

Ever since he'd held her after her ultrasound, when she'd wept for all her parents would miss, there had been a tiny hum of awareness between them.

If she was honest with herself, she'd admit the awareness had been there from the beginning. In her three years at B and A, she'd managed to ignore it. She wasn't the kind of woman he dated. And he certainly wasn't the kind of man she dreamed about.

Their situation was too complicated to add sex to the mix. She knew that. But when he'd walked into the construction trailer this morning, her first, instinctive reaction had been giddiness.

She didn't do giddy.

She usually didn't do stupid, either. But obviously, she was making up for lost time.

You're both adults. He wanted you, too.

It didn't matter. She was pregnant, for God's sake. She wasn't enormous yet, but her body was already ungainly. Swollen. She loved her pregnant belly, and if she and Nick were long-time lovers, she would want to share the changes with him.

But making love with him again? Getting naked, letting him look at her pregnant self? She couldn't do it.

It would let him…assume things.

Things she was unsure of. She still wasn't convinced Nick could give her what she needed—a father for her baby. Steadfast love for both of them.

He'd be around for the week. Seven days. Could she maintain the distance between them for six more days? Keep from falling into the "stupid" trap?

It irritated her that she couldn't immediately answer yes to either of those questions.

She hit the refresh key on her computer too hard as her phone buzzed the arrival of a text message, but she ignored it. Nick was watching her again, and she shoved away from her desk. "I'm going to take a look at the area I've sketched out for a deck. I have some ideas I want to think about."

"I'll go with you." Nick stood, then Mark did as well.

"Me, too."

"Sit down, both of you. I'm going by myself. I need some fresh air." *Need time to think.*

THE TEXT MESSAGE HAD been from Jen, asking if she could meet at the restaurant at four-thirty. Since Jen was her boss, Sierra figured it wasn't a request. So at four o'clock, she closed down her computer, shoved into her briefcase the papers she needed to study that evening, and pushed herself away from her computer.

"You leaving already?" Nick asked.

"Jen wants to meet me."

"I'll see you later, then," he said. His voice was casual. The tone and words a colleague would use at the end of a workday. But his gaze promised that he would seek her out. He probably thought they would pick up where they'd left off earlier.

That wasn't going to happen.

She lifted her briefcase. "See you both tomorrow." She exited the trailer without waiting for a response.

Thirty minutes later, after dropping off her briefcase at her apartment and washing her face, she headed downstairs to Jen's restaurant, still wearing her boots. It took a while to get the boots off, and she was already late. And she planned to head back to the site after they finished talking.

When she walked into The Summer House, Kerry was inserting a list of the day's specials into the menus, and she looked up warily. "Ms. Clark. Have a seat, and I'll tell Jen you're here."

She disappeared into the back, and Sierra sat at a

table. The restaurant was empty of customers, but it buzzed with activity. Waitresses moved around the room, setting out flowers in small vases, napkins and silverware on all the tables. Jen emerged from behind the swinging door, then voices rose in the kitchen behind it. As her boss slid into the chair opposite Sierra's, china shattered in the back with a high-pitched crash. A lot of china.

Jen frowned and half stood, then they heard Kerry's voice. "Okay, Cal, you've had your little hissy fit. I'll take the plates out of your next paycheck. Now get that mess cleaned up." Muttered words sounded, then Kerry's voice again, a little louder. "Cal. Knock it off. Don't make me open a can of whoop-ass on you."

Jen sank back into the chair with a tiny smile. "Thank you, Kerry," she murmured, her eyes twinkling. "The one and only time I've seen her flustered is the day you came to see me," she said to Sierra. "She's worth her price in rubies."

"That's good," Sierra said carefully. "I guess you'll need an assistant for…later."

"That was the idea." Jen straightened. "Thanks for coming here to meet me. I couldn't get away to come to you."

"Not a problem. It's not a long walk." She held herself stiffly in the chair, and Jen touched her hand.

"I need to apologize to you. What I did—insisting on getting Nick back here—was wrong. I embarrassed you and made you uncomfortable. And I let you think I don't trust you."

Sierra lifted one shoulder. "It's your house. You're entitled to do whatever you want."

Jen leaned closer. "Sierra, I'm sorry, all right? I screwed up. How can I make it better? Do you want me to fire Nick? I'll eat the contract, pay him what we owe him and tell him to go."

Sierra took a deep breath, releasing the tension in her shoulders. "No. I gave him a week. By that time, I'll…" She hesitated.

"You'll have the problem solved?"

She hoped she would—both the problem with the thefts and the issues between her and Nick. "Yes."

Jen had dark circles beneath her eyes and looked as if she'd lost weight. Sierra had been so caught up in her own problems she hadn't even noticed. But thinking back, she realized Jen had looked ragged last night, too. "Are you all right?" Her gaze dropped to Jen's abdomen. "Is the baby okay?"

Jen smiled. "I'm fine. I've been worried about Delaney, but she's good now."

"The drummer from that band?"

"Yeah. There was this guy…" She sighed. "How come it's always about a guy? Anyway, her heart was broken, but he figured out a way to fix it. So she's all good again. I should be catching up on my sleep, but now I'm planning a party for them."

Jen pressed her fingers to her eyes. "I think that's why I was so determined to fix whatever is wrong between you and Nick. I saw you with Mark and I was worried." She shrugged. "I couldn't help Delaney. But I thought maybe I could help you." She smiled, but her mouth trembled. "Damn hormones."

"Tell me about it." Sierra slumped against the back of the chair. "They make you do things you wouldn't normally consider."

"Exactly. I can step back and be appalled at myself. But I would probably do it again."

Sierra smiled. "That's honest, anyway."

"So do you and Nick want to come to the party?" Jen watched her carefully.

Sierra clenched her hands in her lap. Jen was inviting them as a couple. Nick had said he wanted to get involved. But did he want to do it publicly?

It was time to test his apparent change of heart. "Yes," she said recklessly. "That sounds great."

She hoped Nick would see it that way.

WHERE THE HELL WAS SHE?

Nick peered into the window of The Summer House one more time, but Sierra wasn't there. He'd left the job site a half hour after she did, hoping to catch up with her after her meeting with Jen. But she wasn't at the restaurant or the Harp. She wasn't at her apartment. He'd seen Jen briefly, and she had no idea where Sierra had gone after their meeting.

He'd walked the whole business district to see if she was in a shop. He felt like a fool, but what if something had happened to her?

Why was her phone turned off? Why hadn't she returned his calls?

He sat on one of the benches on the sidewalk, a couple of stores down from her apartment, and waited. The sky was darkening and it was after eight o'clock when he finally saw her SUV pull into the alley next to her building. A few minutes later, Sierra emerged, carrying a crumpled fast-food bag that she dumped in the trash.

He walked toward her, but before he could speak, she faltered to a halt. "Nick. What are you doing here?"

"Waiting for you." All the worry that had been gnawing at him rose up and spilled over. "Where have you been? I was concerned."

"What? You were worried?"

"I couldn't get you on the phone. I thought something had happened."

"I was at the site," she said with a frown. "You know cell phone reception is sketchy out there. What did you think had happened?"

She looked bewildered, and he flushed. "That you were sick, or something was wrong with the baby," he muttered, feeling like a complete fool.

"Why would you think that?"

"I thought we were getting together. I told you I'd see you later."

"That's a…a generic goodbye," she said, clearly baffled. "It didn't mean we had a date. And I said I'd see you tomorrow."

He opened the door to her vestibule and tried to salvage some of his dignity. "I thought we had things to discuss."

She studied him for a long moment, and he tried not to squirm. "Never mind. I guess we got our signals crossed. What were you doing at the site?"

"Trying to get my ducks in a row. Jen is in a hurry, and I haven't received a shipping confirmation for the shingles we're using, even though they told Mark they'd fax it to us. I tried to get hold of the company, but they were already closed.

"If you wanted to talk to me after work, you should have said something," she finally replied as she pulled her keys out of her purse. "I'm sorry you were worried, although it's odd that the first thing you thought of when you couldn't get hold of me was that something bad had happened. Do women usually sit by the phone, waiting for you to call, and pick up on the first ring?"

"Of course not. But I thought… I'm sorry," he said. "It was an unsettling day. I made some assumptions."

She leaned against the wall. "I did, too. Jen invited us to a party, and I accepted."

This was a test. He jiggled the change in his pocket. He'd never been part of an "us" before. Wasn't sure he wanted to be now. But he'd promised her he'd try. "Good. I like parties."

Her shoulders slumped, as if she'd been tense. "Great. I think it's tomorrow. I'll let you know."

Her hand shook as she inserted the key into the lock. He put his hand over hers. "Let me."

"I can unlock my damn door," she said.

"Of course you can. But let me help."

The lock opened with a click, and she clutched the

keys in her hand. "Good night, Nick," she said. "I'll see you at the site in the morning."

"Can I walk you upstairs?" he said. "You look tired."

She stared at him for a moment. Trying to figure out his motives? Finally, she sighed. "Thanks. It's been a long day."

He wrapped his arm around her waist and walked up the stairs with her. When she unlocked the door, he followed her inside. She glanced at him with a question in her eyes, but turned on the lights and closed the blinds, then collapsed onto the couch.

"We're not discussing anything tonight," she said. "I'm too tired and it's too late."

He sat beside her. "Then I'll just sit with you for a minute." He draped his arm over the back of the couch and took a deep breath and relaxed. When she rested her head inches from his arm, he fought the impulse to pull her close. He didn't want to disturb the moment.

Sitting here with Sierra was comfortable. Peaceful. He could let his guard down.

He never let his guard down. Nick shifted to study her.

"What do you want?" she said, but her voice was faint. Her braid trailed over his arm, and her eyes were closed.

"To get you to bed," he said.

She stilled, then opened her eyes. They were slumberous, whiskey-colored. Seductive.

"That's not on the agenda," she said, her voice husky.

He hadn't meant it that way. But now he could think of nothing else. Her lips were parted, and her chest rose and fell a little faster. He wanted to pull her closer and cover those lips with his mouth. He'd dreamed of her mouth, of how she tasted. He wanted to taste her again.

"I was going to kiss you this morning. You were going to kiss me back."

"No, I wasn't."

She was lying, but before he could prove it to her, she edged away from him. Leaning forward, she tried to stand up, but fell back onto the couch. A muscle clenched in her jaw as she tried again.

It took a moment for him to understand. She was off balance. Ungainly. And the old couch had very soft cushions.

He wrapped his arm around her shoulders and helped her to her feet.

COMPLETELY HUMILIATED, Sierra moved away from Nick's support as soon as she was steady on her feet. "Thank you."

She sounded churlish, but she didn't care. God! One moment he wanted to kiss her, and the next he had to hoist her off the couch. But that would take care of the attraction she'd been fighting. Now he'd see exactly what she was—a fat, waddling, pregnant woman. Certainly not a sexy potential lover.

"You need to leave, Nick," she said without looking at him. "I'm tired. We have to work tomorrow. And it's going to take me a while to get ready for bed."

"Can't you skip all those things women do at night? That ritual?" He smoothed his hand down her braid, making her nerve endings fire wildly, and she pushed him away.

"I'm talking about unlacing my boots and getting undressed," she said wearily. "That's my bedtime ritual nowadays." She waved him toward the door. "Good night."

He didn't move, and finally she turned to look at him. Instead of the distaste and discomfort she expected, she saw understanding. Tenderness, almost. It was unexpected and surprising.

It made her feel lonely. It brought home the fact that she was struggling through this pregnancy alone. Just as she would struggle to raise her child alone.

"I'd like to help you," he said quietly. He held out his hand. "May I?"

"No, you can't help me get undressed." The thought of letting him take off her clothes and reveal her pregnant body made her squirm with embarrassment. "And you could have come up with a more original line."

"At least let me undo the boots."

He seemed sincere. As if he had no other agenda besides taking off her boots. As she stared at him, uncertain, he turned on the hall light that led to the bedroom. "You look skeptical, and I don't blame you. But

I can't bear the thought of you struggling to take those boots off. Please let me help you."

Instead of answering, she headed for the bedroom. She felt him behind her, but he didn't touch her. She sank onto the high, old-fashioned bed and sighed. "Fine. Thank you, Nick. It's getting harder to unlace them and get them off." It was humiliating to admit that her body was getting in the way of doing something so simple.

"I can do that for you." He knelt on the floor and picked up her left foot. He propped it on his leg as he struggled with the knot, and the light from the hall gleamed on his dark hair as he bent over her feet. In the quiet darkness, she could hear him breathing.

It brought back memories of the other time he'd taken off her shoes. Taken care of her.

She pushed the memories away. She didn't want to go there.

He unlaced the boot and loosened it, then tugged it off, along with her sock. He squeezed her foot, and she couldn't stop the tiny moan of pleasure as he massaged away the ache. He lowered himself to the floor, put her foot in his lap and continued the massage. "These boots are so heavy. Why do you wear them?"

"I need them for work. You know that."

"There must be lighter ones." He squeezed the ball of her foot, wriggled each of her toes. "Your foot is swollen."

"That has nothing to do with the shoes. It's because I'm pregnant." Another sexy side effect.

He finished with her left foot, and reached for her

right. His dark head was so close, she could have touched his hair. Found out if it was as soft as it looked.

She closed her eyes to blot out the sight. The intimacy of having him sitting at her feet in her bedroom was muddling her brain. That, and the way his hands were soothing her sore feet, was insidiously seductive.

"Lie back," he murmured as his hands massaged her calf and unknotted her tight muscles. When she hesitated, he eased her down. "Close your eyes. Relax."

She drifted on the edge of sleep as he loosened the muscles of one calf, then the other. Finally, when she had begun to dream, the bed dipped next to her.

"Sierra, wake up," he said softly.

She opened her eyes to find him leaning over her. He had pulled out the band at the end of her braid and was unraveling it. "You don't want to sleep in your clothes. You need to get undressed."

When she struggled to sit up, he put his arm around her and lifted her, as if he'd been doing it from the beginning. "You okay? Do you want me to leave? I'll stay if you want. On the couch," he added hastily.

"Why are you doing this?" she asked.

"Doing what?"

"Helping me with my boots. Massaging my feet. Taking care of me."

He loosened the rest of her braid so the heavy waves hung over her shoulders. "Because you needed help." He brushed her abdomen with a whisper-soft touch. "I had no idea this would make it hard to do things I take for granted." He shrugged self-consciously. "I never thought about it."

"Thank you, Nick. I'm…I'm glad you were here."

"Me, too." He ran his hand over her hair, then stood up. "Come lock the door behind me."

She waited until the door closed down in the vestibule, then struggled out of her clothes and fell into bed. She drifted off to sleep holding on to an image of Nick, massaging her feet.

CHAPTER SIXTEEN

SHE ARRIVED AT THE SITE early the next morning. Her sleep had been restless and full of dreams of Nick, massaging her legs. Kissing her. Touching her. Finally, shortly after dawn, she'd given up and gotten out of bed. Now, holding a cup of herbal tea, she unlocked the trailer in the insubstantial morning light.

As she read her emails and answered the urgent ones, her mind drifted to the previous night. Nick's solicitous concern had been unexpected. She'd been braced for just the opposite—for him to leave with a sigh of relief when she told him to go.

She'd been completely unprepared for what had actually happened. And now she had to reconcile that caring, considerate side of Nick with the man she thought she knew.

In the middle of a job, while trying to figure out who was stealing from them. With Mark and a crew of workmen watching everything.

She needed to figure out what Nick wanted. What she wanted. But she couldn't let their relationship, whatever that was, interfere with finishing this project. Jen was in a hurry. She had six months to move into a new house and have it ready for a baby.

Sierra's job was to make sure that happened as fast as possible.

So she turned on her computer and stored her purse and briefcase. Then she slid into her chair and pulled out the schedules she'd gotten from Vern at the lumberyard yesterday.

By the time another vehicle pulled up, she'd eliminated three people, but there were six who were still possibilities. A door slammed, breaking her concentration, and she swiveled to face the door as footsteps headed up the stairs.

Nick. His tread was lighter than Mark's. Quicker. She took a deep breath and turned back to her lists. What had happened last night had nothing to do with work. Nothing to do with them working together.

Nick stepped inside, and she couldn't stop herself from looking over her shoulder. "Hey," he said. "How do you feel this morning?"

"I'm good. Thanks."

"You sleep okay?"

"Yes." She cleared her throat. "Thank you for… for helping me last night. It was embarrassing, but I'm grateful."

He studied her for a long moment, and she couldn't read his expression. "You shouldn't be embarrassed. I did some research last night. The swollen feet thing is normal. It's probably going to get worse before you give birth."

"That's something to look forward to. Thank you for that encouraging news," she said.

Instead of bristling at her sarcasm, he laughed. "Want to know what else you have to look forward to?"

"No, thank you. I've read the same things, and I'm doing my best to ignore them." She swiveled her chair to face him. "Did you actually buy books about pregnancy?"

"Of course not."

Of course he hadn't. What had she been thinking? She turned back to her computer.

"All the stores were closed by the time I left your place. I looked it up online." She heard the grin in his voice.

"Why?" she said after a moment. "Why the sudden change of heart?"

His smile faded and she saw the resolve in his expression. "I told you I wanted to help you. To do what you needed me to do. Up until yesterday, I had no idea how to do that. You won't ask for anything, so I have to figure it out on my own. But taking your boots off for you? Massaging your feet? I can do that. It was easy enough to figure out other things I can do."

"Such as?" she couldn't stop herself from asking.

"I have a few ideas." He stood up. "I'll run them past you later. Right now, I've got to check on some measurements."

Without waiting for her to answer, he headed for the door of the trailer. How was she supposed to focus on work when he left her hanging like that?

Was he talking about taking off her boots? Or was he willing to give her what she really needed—someone to stand by her? Love her? Be a father to her child? Unsettled and afraid to hope, she followed him out the door.

THE SCENT OF LILACS FROM the garden drifted past Sierra as she sat on the brick patio of Maddie and Quinn's house that evening, watching several kids running through the yard, laughing and yelling to each other. She glanced at Nick in the chair beside her and found him watching the children. Once again, she couldn't read his expression.

"I didn't realize there would be kids here," she murmured.

He took a drink of beer from his bottle, then set it down. "You think that's a problem for me, don't you?"

She shrugged uncomfortably. "I don't want you to think I asked you here to show you a bunch of happy families."

"Why *did* you ask me, then?"

She rubbed one palm down the thigh of her jeans. "Jen invited both of us. I was just passing the invitation on."

He watched her in silence for a moment. "Really? That's all it was?"

Jen was standing with a tall, dark-haired man, and groups of other people sat in the twilight, eating hors d'oeuvres and talking. It was a typical party.

But Sierra had made it into more than that. And if she expected Nick to be honest, she had to be, too. "She invited us as a couple," she blurted. "I almost told her we weren't that, but I guess…I guess I wanted to see if we were. I didn't know it was going to be such a family party. I'm sorry."

He finished his beer and peered at the label. "Nothing wrong with family parties. I'm not allergic to kids. I've actually been to parties where there were people under the age of ten." He stood, tossed the bottle into the recycling bin and said, "That beer was pretty good. I'm going to see if Quinn has any more recommendations."

The baby fluttered as he walked away, and Sierra rested her hand on her belly. She shouldn't have done this. The last time she'd pushed him, he'd run back to Chicago.

As she stared into her ginger ale, someone touched her arm. "Hey, Sierra, come meet Sam. Delaney will be here soon," Jen said. "She was on the phone with her record company, and Sam brought the kids early so she could concentrate."

Nick and Quinn were crouched over the cooler of beer, talking. Jen looped her arm through Sierra's. When she glanced behind her, Jen said, "Nick is fine. You can talk to him anytime."

Sierra wasn't so sure that Nick was fine. He was laughing with Quinn, but Nick was polished enough to be comfortable talking to a virtual stranger. How did he feel about what she'd confessed?

Something had shifted in her last night, and she

wanted to explore it. With him. Right now, though, Nick appeared perfectly happy to explore beer with Quinn instead.

Jen tugged on her arm, and she reluctantly transferred her attention to the tall man introduced as Sam McCabe. When Jen asked how his book was coming, Sierra said, "Are you the Sam McCabe who writes thrillers?"

"That would be me," he said.

"I've read your books. I like them a lot." Sierra forced herself to concentrate on their conversation, but she was aware of Nick behind her. The prickle at the back of her neck told her he was watching.

As she talked to Sam about his latest release, Sam glanced behind her several times. "I'm anxious about Delaney," he finally said apologetically. "She's in some tough negotiations."

When a dark blue truck pulled up and Delaney hopped out, Sam's face lit up. Delaney ran toward him and threw her arms around him. "It's done," she said, hugging him hard. "It's over. They gave me everything I wanted. I just had to throw them a few bones." She kissed Sam as if they'd been apart for months instead of a couple hours.

Sierra backed away from them and looked for Nick. He was talking to Walker now.

She shouldn't have brought him to this party. They should have spent the evening together. Alone. She'd been stupid to try and test him.

After that almost-kiss yesterday, tension had been simmering between them. All today, when she closed her eyes, she'd seen him on the floor at her feet, massaging the aches away. Last night she'd wanted to bury her fingers in his wavy hair and feel the shape of his skull. Next time, would she have the courage to reach for him?

"Isn't it romantic?" Jen murmured beside her, drawing her attention away from Nick. "Those are Sam's niece and nephew, Rennie and Leo." She pointed to a blond boy and a redheaded girl. "Delaney has no idea how this is going to work out. It's complicated and messy and nothing is certain. But she and Sam love each other, so they'll figure out a way to make it happen."

Messy. Complicated. Uncertain. Sierra watched Delaney and Sam, their arms wrapped around each other's waists and their bodies pressed together from shoulder to knee. They both glowed.

That was what Sierra wanted. That kind of love. That kind of need. She wanted to be everything to a man she loved.

She wanted to be everything to Nick. Was she foolish to want that with him? Silly to think he could change that much? Reckless to imagine it was even possible?

Would Nick ever be able to commit to her?

And if he did, would she be willing to accept uncertainty and messiness as the price?

NICK SLOUCHED AGAINST the side of the house and watched the couple on the patio. Delaney was plastered against the guy, and two of the kids had run up and thrown their arms around her. He didn't know Delaney, other than as the drummer at the pub, but he fought the lump forming in his throat as he watched her with the man and the kids.

She was incandescent. Glowing with happiness. It was a shocking change from the last time he'd seen her, performing in the pub. Delaney had smiled and talked, but her eyes had been shadowed with sadness.

Now, curved against the man and holding on to the kids, she looked like a different woman. Alive. Radiant. Bursting with love.

It was enough to make even the most jaded cynic envy them. He glanced at Sierra and saw her biting her lip. Was she trying not to cry?

Every person at the party was watching with a smile on their face. He would have bet money there wasn't a dry female tear duct in the crowd. Even some of the men were pretending they'd gotten something in their eye.

One person stepped forward, then another. Soon, almost everyone was crowded around the family, asking questions, giving them hugs. Sierra had told him, on the way to the party, that Delaney and the guy had had a hard time working things out.

This wasn't just a man and a woman privately solving their problems, he realized. Everyone in the crowd clearly knew what had happened with the couple. Judging from the smiles on everyone's faces, they were all thrilled for them.

A couple of months ago, it would have made Nick crazy to have a whole town knowing his business.

Tonight, watching these people celebrating with their friend, it made him feel lonely.

If he overcame huge obstacles to get his heart's desire, who would celebrate with him? His coworkers? His friends in the Chicago business community?

His admin, Janet?

They would be happy for him. Pleased. But they'd clap him on the back, say, "Good for you, man," then continue on with their lives. It would leave no lasting mark on anyone.

He would leave no lasting mark, other than the buildings he'd designed.

It was a hell of a thing to realize.

Nick glanced at Sierra, standing off to the side by herself. Emotion had always equaled weakness for him. He thought he was protecting himself by refusing to feel anything for anyone. But he was really only isolating himself. Cutting himself off from other people. Building a box around his heart.

Sierra told him she'd asked him to this party as a test, and it had pissed him off. But maybe she was right to test him. This was completely new territory for him.

A small part of him wondered how long it would take to earn her trust.

When Jen approached Sierra again, he felt like an outsider as he watched the two women talk. An intruder. Then Sierra turned to him with a smile. "Isn't it great, Nick?"

"Isn't what great?"

Her smile dimmed. "Delaney and Sam. Jen was telling me their story."

"They look really happy. I'm glad for them."

"But you don't believe in happily ever after, do you?" she murmured. "I almost forgot."

He wanted to tell her she'd drawn the wrong conclusion. That instead of the cynicism she expected, he was feeling a little lost. A lot alone. But the chance slipped away when everyone's attention turned to the couple again. Delaney and Sam still hadn't let go of each other. They looked like they never would.

How did you get a relationship like that? Was that what Nick wanted with Sierra?

The idea of opening himself to her, of exposing the man behind the face he showed to the world, was terrifying. Would he have the courage to do it?

And if he did, would Sierra accept him, flaws and all?

Or was she still looking for perfection?

NICK DRANK A TOAST, MET Sam McCabe, and talked to the happy couple for a while, but he felt like an imposter in this crowd of joyful people. Everyone was connected, with a partner, with their kids. He was here with Sierra, but she was still blocking him out. He hadn't given her what she needed.

Jen was setting out the food, and Walker was helping her. He tried to get her to sit down and let him carry the dishes from the kitchen, but she laughed at him as she walked back into the house.

Delaney and Sam were completely sappy in their happiness. Other couples stood talking, husbands and wives holding hands.

Sierra was speaking to Maddie, apparently comparing pregnancy stories, judging by the way they touched each other's abdomens. "Hey, Nick," Quinn said from behind him. "How about another beer?"

"I'm good. But thanks," he said as the other man pulled another bottle of water out of a cooler.

Quinn took a long drink of water as he stood next to Nick, watching the two women. "Scary as hell, isn't it?"

"What?" Nick asked cautiously.

Quinn gave him a surprised look. "Having a baby. Being a father."

"Yeah, it is." Nick finished his beer in one gulp. "Maybe I will have another."

Quinn laughed. "When Maddie told me she was pregnant, I wanted a Jameson's really bad." He finished his water and tossed the bottle into a bin. "I've got to make sure she sits down. She's been standing way too long."

As Quinn drew his wife away, Nick moved toward Sierra. "How are you doing?" he murmured.

"I'm good," she answered with a puzzled look, as if she was surprised he'd asked. "Are you okay?"

"I'm fine," he said. "Let's have some food, then get out of here."

She nodded. "Okay. I'm a little tired."

After eating quickly and saying goodbye to their

friends, they got into Nick's car and drove toward town. Twilight had deepened into darkness, and there were few other cars on the road.

"I was an ass tonight," Nick said abruptly. "I walked away from you in the middle of the party."

She tucked her fingers beneath her thighs. "I shouldn't have made it a test for you. I'm sorry."

"I don't know about being a couple, Sierra. Everyone there was connected, and they all looked happy about it. But…"

"But you don't know if you can do that," she finished quietly.

"I want to be what you need," he said. "I'm trying to. But I don't know if I can open up as much as you want me to."

She shifted in the seat, and her face was pale in the darkness. "That's honest," she said quietly. "We can go slowly."

Nick took her hand, and her fingers curled around his. Something inside him loosened. "Okay. Slow is good," he said.

Neither of them spoke as they drove into town. He parked at the curb in front of her apartment and helped her out. "I have to go back to Chicago for the weekend," he said. "Some of my current projects need attention. Are you going to be all right for a couple of days?"

"I'll be fine," she said. Her shoulders seemed to relax. "I know you can't spend all your time up here. You have a business to run." She absently rubbed the back of his hand with her thumb. "I have a lot to do at the work site, anyway. I'm determined to figure out who is behind our problems."

"Don't take any stupid chances," he said, tightening his grip on her hand. "Promise me."

"I won't do anything stupid," she assured him. "I'm going to call some of the carpenters' references and talk to Vern at the lumberyard. That's all."

Her face was pale in the moonlight, and her hair curled around her face. He wanted to tangle his hands in those curls and kiss her. To pull her against him and spend a long time tasting her. "I don't want to leave," he murmured.

"You have responsibilities in Chicago," she said. "I understand that."

He'd meant he didn't want to leave her tonight. But apparently Sierra wasn't ready for that.

Maybe he wasn't, either. Maybe he needed to figure out what he wanted before they took that step. "I'll see you on Monday," he said.

CHAPTER SEVENTEEN

NICK DROVE A LITTLE TOO fast down the dirt road leading to the work site, wincing when he couldn't avoid one of the ruts. Since he was going to spend more time here, he was already researching different vehicles. The sleek sports car was fun in the city, but not very practical here in the country.

His chest muscles relaxed when he spotted lights inside the trailer and Sierra's SUV parked next to it. When he'd stopped by her apartment and she hadn't answered the buzzer, he'd figured she was out here. But he couldn't banish the worry that crept in. It was barely sunrise. She should still be sleeping.

Parking beside her car, he grabbed the plastic bag from the seat next to him and hurried up the steps. Before he reached the top, she opened the door.

"Nick!" She stepped aside so he could enter the trailer. "What are you doing here?" There were dark circles beneath her eyes and she hadn't braided her hair.

He wanted to sweep her into his arms, but he shrugged and said, "This is where I work."

Her face a careful mask, she closed the door and

leaned against it. "When did you get back in town? Last night?"

She sounded disappointed, as if she'd been waiting for him, and he took a step closer. Then stopped. "Just now," he said.

"You drove here overnight and you came right to work? You must be exhausted."

He drew a deep breath. Over the long weekend, he'd understood he needed to be more open with Sierra. "I had a nap in a rest area. I'm tired, but I wanted to see how you were doing. When you weren't at your apartment, I figured you must be out here."

"I'm fine. I'm here because there's a lot to do and I wasn't sleeping well." Her hands trembled, and she laced them together. Was it from lack of sleep, or was she nervous?

"I thought about you over the weekend, Sierra," he said, holding her gaze. "I got something for you."

Nick watched, fascinated, as color washed Sierra's face. Her eyelids were slumberous and her hair was a wild mass down her back, although it was obvious she'd tried to tame it.

He picked up the bag he'd dropped on the floor, and handed it to her. "See how these work for you."

She opened the sack and pulled out a shoe box. Giving him a puzzled look, she removed the lid. As she lifted out the high-tech, lightweight boots, he suddenly felt stupid. He'd gotten boots for a pregnant woman who was probably already self-conscious about her looks. What kind of dumb-ass gift was that?

As she examined them, turned them in her hands, hefted them to test their weight, her eyes filled with tears. He shoved his hands into his pockets, wishing he could snatch them back and erase them from her memory.

"You got me new boots." Her voice was soft with wonder, and her eyes swam as she looked up at him. "The right size. They're so light. And easy to put on." She sniffled. "This is the best present anyone's ever given me."

"You've gotten some pretty lame gifts, then," he muttered.

She dropped the boots and threw herself at him, wrapping her arms around his waist. "You thought about what I needed," she said, her voice fierce. "You figured out what would work. You went out of your way to find them." She reached up and cupped his face. "Thank you, Nick."

"You're welcome." Heat crept up his cheeks. "It's not a big deal."

"It's a very big deal." She let him go and sat in her chair to put the boots on. When she stood, she rocked back and forth a few times, then walked around the trailer.

She stopped in front of him, grinning. "They're perfect. They feel so good—like I don't even have to break them in. And so light. Thank you."

He watched her admire the boots. "Now I guess I won't have any excuse to help you take them off."

She lifted her head to meet his gaze. "I loved

watching you undo my boots," she said in a low voice. "And your foot massage. I loved that, too."

"Yeah? Then I guess I'm good for something." Neither of them looked away. In the silence, he heard waves crashing onto the beach. Birds sang in the trees surrounding the lot. His heart beat heavily in his chest.

Deep in the whiskey-colored depths of her eyes, hunger stirred. He watched it, fascinated, as his own hunger leaped to life. Hunger that was always there, humming below the surface.

Sierra curled her toes in her new boots as she watched Nick. She'd thought about him all weekend. Wished she'd kissed him before he left. Wished they'd done more than kiss.

Nothing was decided. Nick wasn't sure if he could be what she needed, and neither was she. But he'd brought her boots. She wanted him. And he wanted her.

"Sierra," he murmured. His mouth touched hers tentatively, as if afraid she'd back away.

If she had a brain in her head, she would. But she leaned against him, deepening the kiss. His arms came around her immediately, pulling her snug against him, and she twined hers around his neck. His hair was as soft as she imagined it would be, and he groaned when she tunneled her fingers through it.

He slanted his mouth over hers and kissed her harder, and she opened for him. He savored her, stroking his tongue over hers as if memorizing her flavor, learning every inch of her mouth.

He caressed her as they kissed, his fingers roaming from her shoulder to her hip. His hands trembled as he skimmed the sides of her breasts.

When she shuddered against him, he cupped her breast, and her nipple hardened against his palm. His kiss deepened and tasted of desperation. Need. Urgency.

She yanked his shirt from the waistband of his jeans and slid her hands beneath it. His skin was hot over his tense muscles, and soft hair slid through her fingers as she touched his nipples. Satisfaction surged through her when she felt them harden.

With an inarticulate cry, he burrowed beneath her sweater and made an impatient noise when he found her T-shirt. Moments later, his hands were on her skin. His callused fingertips scraped over her, making her shiver. When he cupped her breasts, she moaned into his mouth and sat heavily on the desk, her legs trembling too much to support her.

"Sierra," he whispered as he pushed her sweater and T-shirt up to her neck. Before she had a chance to become self-conscious about her ugly maternity jeans, he'd opened her bra and taken her breasts in his hands.

"You're beautiful," he murmured as he caressed her. He touched her nipple, and she sucked in a breath and flinched.

He froze. "Did I hurt you?"

"No," she managed to say. "They're very sensitive."

"Okay." He fumbled at her back and rehooked her bra, then smoothed her shirt and sweater down as she opened her eyes.

"Nick." She trapped his hands against her. "I didn't mean I wanted you to stop. I wanted you to…" She felt her cheeks redden. "I meant it felt good. More intense. More arousing." She swallowed, desire still an aching need inside her. "Touch me again. Please."

He put his hands over her once more and kissed her deeply. His thumbs brushed her, and even through her sweater it made her cry out. "Nick! Please!"

His hands tightened, then he pulled her against him. His erection strained against her belly, and his palms roamed over her back. He kissed her again, then eased her away.

"You're killing me, Sierra," he muttered, his forehead against hers. "I want to peel off your clothes and kiss every inch of you. I want to watch you as I touch your sensitive breasts.

"But I'm not going to make love to you on top of a desk. In a construction trailer." He let her go slowly, each finger sliding away individually. His smile was shaky. "At least not the first few dozen times."

"And after that?" she managed to say.

"All bets are off."

The baby moved, and she smoothed her hand over her belly. They wouldn't be making love on a desk anytime soon.

A truck door slammed outside the trailer. They had company. Nick straightened her sweater, tucked his shirt into his jeans and smoothed her hair. "Tonight," he whispered, "we'll go on a date. All right?"

He wanted to take her on a date. Warmth bloomed in Sierra's chest, and she nodded. Then, as footsteps started up the stairs, she slid into her desk chair and turned blindly to her computer. Nick picked up the shoe box and put her old boots inside, then shoved them beneath his desk. "I'm going to get some sleep," he said, smoothing a hand down her hair. "I'll see you this afternoon."

"Okay," she said, her heart still racing.

Mark opened the door, and Nick nodded. "Just got back from Chicago and checking in," he said. "I'll see you later."

Nick's car rumbled to life, the sound fading as he drove off. When it was quiet again, the contractor said, "You guys got here early."

"I was here before six. Nick showed up a few minutes ago." Long enough to leave her breathless and wanting.

Mark looked over her shoulder at the schedules she had on her desk and the notes from her conversations with the workers' references. "You make any progress with that?"

"I think so. There are two carpenters I'm focusing on. And a few guys from the lumberyard."

"Who are the carpenters?"

She took a deep breath. "I'd rather not say. You work with these guys all the time. I don't want to make any unfounded accusations."

He held her gaze for a moment, then nodded. There was a shadow in his eyes as he looked away. Did he suspect, too?

SHE WATCHED THE CARPENTERS all morning, wondering if she was right. A delivery of plywood for the outside walls of the house was due this afternoon, and she was going to pay attention to who signed for it. And who delivered it.

She was on hold with the company supplying their shingles when she heard Nick's car. She swiveled in her chair and smiled as he walked in. He stopped in the doorway, then closed the door behind him and kissed her.

Before she could sink into the kiss, he moved to his desk and dropped his briefcase. "I'm on hold with the shingle people," she said.

"Problem?"

"I hope not. They're getting cold feet about letting us have the solar ones. They're still experimental, the regional sales manager says, and claims they don't have enough stock."

"Is that Rich Salazar?"

"Yes. We've already sent him a deposit, and now he's trying to back out."

"I know him. Want me to talk to him?"

"I can handle it."

Nick's expression froze for a moment. "Okay. Let me know if you need help."

Accepting help from him wasn't admitting weakness.

He knew a lot of people in the business. If he could convince that weasel Salazar to give her the shingles, she should let him. "Nick, I'm…"

She heard a truck rumbling down the road, and she held the phone to her ear as she watched it arrive. It was the plywood. And one of her two suspects hurried over to accept the delivery even before the truck stopped.

Almost as if Kyle had been waiting for the guy.

Sierra glanced at Mark, sorry about what was going to happen next. She'd noticed a little tension between the two men, but Mark looked out for his brother. He was going to be devastated.

Kyle signed the invoice, then glanced around. Before he handed the clipboard back to the driver, he pulled what looked like a wad of cash from beneath the clip and shoved it into his pocket.

Sierra memorized the driver's face and scribbled down the truck number, then dropped the phone on her desk and watched Kyle stroll back to the framed-out house, swinging his hammer back and forth. As the truck pulled away, Sierra ran out of the trailer.

"Kyle, I need to speak with you, please," she called as she walked toward him.

He froze, then glanced over his shoulder. He must have seen the suspicion on her face, because he dropped the hammer and raced toward the trees at the back of the property.

She ran after him. "Kyle, stop. I just want to talk to you."

He ran faster, and she followed him into the grove. He

glanced back as he crashed through the undergrowth, but kept going.

As she followed him, her toe hit something solid and she stumbled forward. She grabbed for a handhold, but her fingers slid off the slippery bark of a birch tree, and she went down hard—her belly hitting a piece of concrete. Pain, fierce and terrifying, shot through her. As she rolled to the side, her hands already reaching for her abdomen, she barely noticed the other pain in her thigh.

"SIERRA?" NICK CALLED as she dropped the phone on her desk and flew out the door. As he followed her out, he saw the delivery truck pulling away and one of the carpenters fleeing into the woods. Sierra was running full speed after him.

"Damn it, Sierra, wait a minute," he called. But she either didn't hear him or didn't intend to stop, because she kept going. As she disappeared into the stand of birch and maple trees, he took off after her.

When he reached the grove, he heard a rustling sound, but didn't see her or the carpenter. "Where are you?" he called.

"Nick?" She sounded weak, as if she was out of breath. "I'm over here. In the trees."

He hurried toward the sound of her voice and saw her lying propped against a tree, her hands on her stomach. He began to run.

Her eyes were closed and she was drawing in deep

breaths. He crouched beside her. "What happened? Did he hurt you? Are you okay?"

She opened her eyes, and her fear made his own gut clench. "Tripped on a chunk of concrete." Her booted foot nudged at a solid mass hidden by some ferns. "This stuff wasn't here a few days ago. Someone must have dumped it."

She sucked in a breath and grabbed his sleeve. "I landed on my belly, and it hurts," she panted. "Oh, God, Nick. It hurts."

"Is the baby all right?"

"I don't know."

He lifted her shirt and saw a dark line of bruises already forming below her navel. He put his hand there, not sure what he would feel. "What?" she said. "What's wrong?"

"You're bruised." He lowered her shirt. "Let's get you to the hospital."

As he lifted her off the ground, he saw the gash in her leg. Blood poured out of it, saturating the dead leaves next to her. "Oh my God."

Setting her down again, he yanked his belt out of the loops on his jeans and slid it around her thigh, pulling it tight.

"You cut your leg, too."

Blood continued to seep sluggishly out of the cut in her jeans, even with the tourniquet. Dread rolled through him. "What the hell were you thinking, Sierra?" He picked her up and headed for his car. "Why were you running after that kid?"

"I…I didn't think," she said. "I saw the driver give Kyle money, and went outside to confront him."

"I was right there, Sierra. So was Cameron. You didn't think to ask us for help?"

"Why are you yelling at me?" She gripped the collar of his sweater behind his neck. "I made a mistake." Her voice caught. "And I haven't felt the baby move since I hit the concrete."

Nick's anger vanished, replaced by terror. "He doesn't move all the time, does he? He's probably okay." He eased her belly closer to his chest as he half walked, half ran toward his car. "Women must fall when they're pregnant." *Not onto a sharp piece of concrete.* "Your body is engineered for that."

She clutched him more tightly. "You're such an architect." He heard tears in her voice.

He ran faster for his car as Mark hurried down the stairs. "What happened?"

"She was chasing the guy who's been stealing from us and she fell. It was your brother." Nick opened the sports car and slid her inside. "I'm taking her to the hospital."

As soon as he got in the vehicle, Sierra reached for his hand and gripped it tightly. He squeezed hard, then had to let her go as he maneuvered his sports car through the ruts in the lane. He cursed himself for having such an impractical car. He should have gotten something else already.

"Do you have a towel?" Sierra asked. "I'm bleeding

all over your seat." Her breath hitched. "And onto my new boots."

"I don't give a damn about the seat, and I'll get you a new pair of boots." The blood was flowing a little faster. "Tighten the belt a notch."

Her hands fumbled as she loosened it, then pulled it tighter. He emerged from the tracks in the mud onto the main road and put the pedal to the floor.

"THE BABY'S STILL NOT moving," she whispered forty-five minutes later.

Nick looked at the IV line attached to her hand, the belt around her abdomen that was hooked up to a machine, the stylus that was moving up and down on the paper, registering the baby's heartbeat. "His heart's beating. I can see the tracing."

Sierra clung to Nick's hand, as she'd done since they'd taken her out of the car and put her on a gurney. Now she was lying on a bed in a cubicle in the Sturgeon Falls hospital emergency room, surrounded by machines. They'd removed her bloodstained clothes and replaced them with a hospital gown that was tucked up over her belly. A blue drape was arranged over her legs, and a surgeon was stitching the gash.

There was barely room to stand next to her. Nick felt helpless. Lost. Terrified.

No one had told them a thing about the baby. They'd hooked Sierra up to that machine, seen that the baby's heart was beating, and left her with the surgeon.

The doctor was putting the last layer of sutures into

her leg. "You've lost a lot of blood," he said without looking up. "You might need a transfusion. We'll see what your blood count looks like."

"A transfusion?" she echoed. Her face got even whiter. "Can they do that if I'm pregnant?"

"They may not have to do it. The fluids might be enough."

Nick noticed that he hadn't answered her question.

"I thought they'd do an ultrasound right away," Sierra said.

"Nope. This was more urgent. You were losing blood too fast." He tied off the last suture, snipped the end and leaned back as if to admire his work. "You need to stay off this for twenty-four hours, at least, but that shouldn't be a problem. They'll want to keep you tonight." He glanced at Nick. "I'll need to see her in my office in five days, to check how she's doing."

"Hey, I can hear, too," she said.

A red flush crept up the older surgeon's neck. "Sorry. I assumed your husband would be driving you," he muttered.

Nick opened his mouth to correct the guy, then closed it again. His assumptions didn't matter. It wasn't the doctor's business who he was to Sierra.

Husband. He'd never thought of himself as a husband. Or a father. The words were foreign. A few months ago, they would have terrified him. But they were only words. He'd felt true terror this afternoon, when he'd seen Sierra on the ground holding her belly, with blood pouring from her leg.

He gripped her fingers more tightly and put his free hand over hers. They stayed that way, with both hands entwined, as the doctor bandaged her leg.

When he finished, he pulled back the curtain to reveal a technician waiting with a familiar-looking machine. An ultrasound. Nick leaned closer to Sierra, needing to protect her, as dread twisted his stomach. If the baby's heart was beating, why couldn't she feel him moving?

What if the baby died? His stomach felt hollow, his chest too heavy. Ever since that first ultrasound, the child had been real to Nick.

Sierra *couldn't* lose this baby. Not after losing her parents.

He held his breath as the technician put the wand on Sierra's belly. The screen was black for a moment, then the baby appeared.

Bigger than the last time. He had his thumb in his mouth, but it looked as if he was just floating. "He's not moving," Nick said, his voice hoarse.

The technician glanced at him. "He's sleeping, Dad." She moved the wand around, got different views, clicked at different points. Very much like the last time. But the last time, Nick hadn't been holding his breath.

Last time, he hadn't been afraid his baby was going to die.

CHAPTER EIGHTEEN

SIERRA'S JAW WAS CLENCHED as she stared at the screen. When he tucked her hair behind her ear, he felt her pulse racing in her neck. Panicked. He needed to distract her. "They took your hair down while they were checking your head," he said softly. "Let me fix it."

He pulled the loose strands together and began braiding. They flowed like a silken river through his fingers as he wound them together. When he finished, he picked up a rubber band off the ultrasound cart and fastened the ends together.

"Thank you," Sierra murmured. She took her eyes off the screen to glance up at him. "Where did you learn to braid hair?"

The ultrasound technician gave him a short, approving nod. *"Take care of her,"* she mouthed.

His hands froze. Did that mean she'd seen something bad?

"Nick? What's wrong?" Panic filled Sierra's voice again.

"Nothing, sweetheart. What did you ask me?"

"Where did you learn to braid?"

"I went to camp one summer," Nick said. "We had to

braid those lame plastic things that you were supposed to hang around your neck." He forced himself to keep his eyes on her and not on the screen. Why had the technician wanted him to take care of Sierra? Was something wrong? Was there something that had alarmed her? Something she didn't want Sierra to see?

"I always wanted to go to summer camp. Was it fun?"

"I'll tell you about it later." The words slipped out before he realized it, and he wanted to snatch them back.

No. He'd have to tell her sooner or later. She'd have to know what she was risking, if she wanted him to stay.

She held his gaze. "Okay," she said softly.

He had to look back at the screen, but nothing seemed different. After five agonizingly long minutes, the technician nodded. "I'll get this to the radiologist right away. He'll come back to talk to you as soon as he can."

"Wait a minute," Nick said. "What did you see? Is there a problem?"

"The radiologist will be by to talk to you," she repeated. "I'm not allowed to tell you anything."

"Just tell us if there's something wrong with our baby."

"I'm sorry, sir, but you're going to have to wait."

"Wait?" He let go of Sierra's hand. "You expect us to just sit here and worry? That's bullshit. Tell us now."

"I'm sorry," she said quietly. "I can't. You'll have to wait." She rolled her machine out of the cubicle, leaving him alone with Sierra.

He looked at the monitor, and saw the stylus moving. "His heartbeat looks the same," Nick said, trying to sound cheerful. Upbeat. Damn hard, when it felt as if his heart had been wrenched out of his chest. "We're getting way ahead of ourselves."

"She's going to die," Sierra whispered, her mouth trembling. "And it will be my fault."

Why didn't you ask me for help instead of running through the woods yourself? Nick struggled to bury the anger. It wouldn't help them now.

"I ran after Kyle," she sobbed, "and now our baby is going to die." Tears poured down her face.

Our baby. It was the first time she said that. She always called it *her* baby.

"He's not going to die," Nick said. "If he was going to, he would have already." He had no idea if that was true or not, but he couldn't let her lie there, thinking she had killed her child. "That technician was just mean."

Sierra shifted her hand and gripped his more tightly. "You keep calling the baby *he.* I keep calling it *her.* Do you think it's a boy?"

"Do you want a girl?"

Tears welled in her eyes again. "I want a healthy baby," she sobbed. "That's all."

"We're going to have a healthy baby," he said. Sierra's hand tightened on his, suddenly hopeful. *We.* He'd said *we* were going to have a healthy baby.

Not Sierra alone. Both of them.

Whatever happened, it would happen to him as much as Sierra.

He glanced at the heart rate monitor again. Nothing had changed. God, the baby had to be okay. He wouldn't be able to bear it if they lost him.

Nick thought he'd banished the fear that had settled on his shoulders so long ago. The fear of losing someone he cared about. But it had dug its claws into him again, and the pain was tearing him apart.

He brushed damp hair away from Sierra's face and used some of the rough tissues from the box on the counter to blot up the tears. "Don't cry, sweetheart," he murmured. How was he going to distract her? "I'll tell you about camp while we wait for the doctor."

He swallowed. This was it. Truth time. He was doing more here than distracting Sierra. He was ripping the curtains away from his past and exposing it to her.

"I went to camp one summer with my next-door neighbor," he began. "His parents were sending him, and I was living with them, so they sent me, too."

Some of the fear in her expression was replaced by curiosity. "Why were you living with your neighbor?"

"My mother took off when I was twelve." He stared at the green drape concealing them from the corridor, and realized he couldn't clearly remember what she looked like. "She left me with a neighbor and said she'd be back in a couple days. I never saw her again."

"Oh my God. Nick." Sierra propped herself on one elbow and reached for him. He wrapped his arm around her and urged her to lie down again. He hugged her for a moment as she twined her arms around his neck and held him tightly.

"That's horrible," she said into his neck. "How could anyone do that to their child?"

A wave of shame washed over him. He'd abandoned her when she'd told him she was pregnant. But he was trying to make amends. He wasn't going to leave her again.

He interlaced his fingers with hers and eased away. He had to tell her the rest. "Mrs. Kelly was a kind woman, and her son was my best friend. She kept me as long as she could, but her husband was laid off and money got tight. So she had to call children's services. They put me in a foster home.

"I was an angry kid, and I went through about ten of them before I turned eighteen. I lost count after a while. Some of them were okay, some of them weren't." The bad ones, the ones that still gave him nightmares, were memories he kept tightly locked away. "I got good grades in high school, because I knew it was my way out. I made it through college on scholarships and loans, and after I got my degree, I got a job at a small firm. Eventually, I left and started B and A."

Sierra clung to his hands. "Did you ever find your mother?" she asked quietly.

"I never looked. Every once in a while I think about hiring a private investigator, but I've never done it." He glanced at her then, to find her gaze riveted on him, her eyes pools of sympathy. "I guess I don't really want to know. Maybe she was killed in an accident of some kind. Maybe that's why she didn't come back." He pleated the blanket beneath his fingers. "I'd rather imagine she was dead than have to accept that she walked away from me and never looked back."

"Thank you for sharing that with me," Sierra finally said. "I think...I think you don't tell many people."

"You're the first." His leg jittered as he waited for her to say something more.

She struggled to sit up. "You've never let anyone else get close, have you? You're afraid of being abandoned again."

"I don't *want* anyone to get close. Or at least I never did before. I'm a bad risk," he said. "I never knew my father—he took off before I was born. And even before my mother left, she was no prize. She liked to party a lot more than she liked having a kid. I have no idea how to be a father. No idea how to raise a child. All I know are lots of ways *not* to do it."

Sierra put her hands on his face. "Listen to me, Nick Boone," she said fiercely. "You're a good man. You'll be a good father. Our baby needs you. *I* need you."

"Do you?" he murmured, as the memory of her flying out of the trailer, alone, replayed in his head.

Before she could ask what he meant, the curtain opened and a middle-aged man in scrubs moved to the end of the bed. As he consulted his notes, she clung to Nick's hand.

She was gripping so hard it hurt, and her face was ashen with fear.

"I'm Dr. Moore, the radiologist," the doctor said. He glanced at the heart rate monitor and nodded. "On the sonogram, I don't see any problems with your baby."

He lifted her gown and studied the darkening bruises across her abdomen. "But you took a bad fall. I'm worried about the placenta."

"What…what about the placenta?" she asked, clutching Nick's shirt with her other hand.

"A fall like that can make it separate from the uterus. I'm concerned about a tiny area I saw on the ultrasound. It could be nothing, or it could be the beginning of a tear. We'll do ultrasounds throughout the night, every couple of hours, to keep track of it."

"What if…" She cleared her throat. "What if the placenta tears?"

"Bed rest in the best-case scenario. Worse-case, we have to deliver the baby."

"How soon will you know?" Nick asked.

"If it's a tear, it will get bigger. We should know by tomorrow. We're going to admit you to the maternity floor as soon as they get a bed ready." He drew the curtain again, and they were alone.

Nick's hand was clammy against hers. "Bed rest. It won't be too bad." He smiled, hoping it hid the sick fear he was feeling. "A life of leisure for a few months."

He was doing a piss-poor job trying to cheer her up, because she reached for his shirt and pulled him close, then sobbed against his chest. He wrapped one arm around her and held her tight, his free hand rubbing her back.

THE ROOM THEY'D WHEELED Sierra to was sickeningly cheerful. The yellow wallpaper had little bunches of purple flowers, and the beds had actual quilts instead of coarse hospital blankets. There was a small bouquet of fresh flowers on the night table, and a tiny bassinet on wheels sat next to the bed.

Nick wanted to smash it into a million pieces. One of the nurses saw him looking at it, and quickly wheeled it out, but it was too late.

Sierra had seen it.

She swallowed once, then again, and her lip trembled. But she held back the tears. "I…I think maybe she moved."

His heart leaped. "Yeah?" He put his hand over hers on her abdomen. "Here?"

"Yes." She shifted her hand and put it over his, pressing his fingers into her firm belly. "There. Did you feel that?"

"No." He willed his fingertips to feel something, anything, but all he felt was the heat from Sierra's skin.

"It was a tiny flutter," she whispered. "But more than before."

"Hey, it's nighttime. He's probably sound asleep." Oh God, that was really lame.

But Sierra nodded. "Probably," she whispered. She brought Nick's hand to her mouth and kissed it. He touched her lips, finding them dry.

He grabbed the glass of water the nurse had left. "Have a drink."

She sipped from the straw, then closed her eyes. Was she tired, or did she want to be alone? How the hell was he supposed to tell? Did she want him to go?

"Sierra?" He waited until she opened her eyes. "Do you want me to leave?"

"No!" She grabbed his shirt again. "Please stay, Nick. I...I need you here."

The fist around his chest loosened. She needed him. "I'm not going anywhere."

A few minutes later, a technician rolled another ultrasound machine into the room. "Time for another one," she said. She worked efficiently, and it took only five minutes for her to finish.

"What do you see?" he asked, knowing it was probably futile.

"One of the doctors will be in to talk to you," she murmured, wheeling the machine out of the room before he could say anything else.

It took only fifteen minutes this time for a harried-looking doctor to come by and tell them that everything looked the same. "Any questions?" she asked. They'd barely shaken their heads when she said, "Great. I've got a baby almost ready to be delivered. They'll do another sonogram in an hour or so."

"Thank you," Sierra murmured, but she had already left.

The wheels of a gurney clattered down the hall, and Nick saw a familiar-looking redhead lying on it. The bartender from the Harp was walking next to her, holding her hand.

"Murphy?" Nick said.

The guy turned to look at him and slowed. "Boone. Sierra. What are you guys doing here?"

"She fell."

The redhead turned to look. "Is she okay?"

"Waiting to see," Nick answered.

He watched as Murphy disappeared around a corner with his wife. Ten minutes later, Jen Barnes appeared in the door.

"Sierra? Nick? What's going on?"

Nick moved closer to Sierra. "She fell. They're doing ultrasounds to make sure everything is okay." He couldn't force himself to say "the baby." It made it too personal. Too scary. He needed to be strong right now.

"May I come in?"

Nick glanced at Sierra, who nodded. He moved to the side, but kept hold of her hand.

Jen's gaze drifted over their joined hands. "What happened?"

Sierra's mouth quivered for a moment, then she swallowed and explained.

"Mark Cameron's brother was the one switching out the wood?" Jen asked.

"Yes."

"Poor Mark," she murmured. "Poor Kyle. He must be in some kind of trouble."

That was Jen's reaction? Nick stared at her in disbelief. He wanted to throw the bastard in jail. Hell, the kid was probably the one responsible for the concrete Sierra had tripped on.

"Maddie fell once, a few months ago," Jen was saying. "It was at the pub. Someone spilled a beer and didn't say anything. She slid and hit the floor really hard. They did the same thing, a bunch of ultrasounds. They scared the crap out of her, too, but everything was all right."

Delaney appeared at the door. "Quinn told us you were here. How are you doing? Is there anything you need? Anything we can get you?"

"I'm good," Sierra said. She scooted up in bed a little. "Is Maddie in labor?"

Jen and Delaney both began talking about how she'd gone into labor six hours ago at the Harp, and Quinn had closed it down. Nick saw some of the tension drain from Sierra's shoulders. Several minutes later, she actually smiled. She still gripped his hand, but her grip wasn't nearly as desperate. Now she threaded her fingers through his and just held on.

Walker and Sam had joined the women, and the room was crowded. Sierra had been in this town for only a short time, but she was part of the community. People knew who she was. She had friends.

She belonged.

Nick wanted this. He wanted to be part of this circle of couples. This community.

Sierra claimed she wanted that, too. But he wasn't so sure anymore.

Ninety minutes later, Walker rushed into the room. "Quinn just came out. Maddie had the baby. It's a girl."

Everyone rushed for the door, but Walker held up his hand. "No hurry. He said it would be a while."

Nick eased into the corner, feeling like an intruder. They smiled at him, acted as if he was included, but he knew the truth. He hadn't forged bonds in this town, as Sierra had. He was on the outside of this group, looking in.

Just like he was always on the outside. Up until now, it had been his choice. And now that he wanted to lower the walls, he realized Sierra hadn't lowered hers.

Just then Quinn walked in, wearing a long blue gown and a blue cap on his head. He held a tiny bundle in his arms and had a huge grin on his face.

"Meet Grace Madeline Murphy," he said.

Everyone else crowded around, and Sierra again tried to sit up in the bed. As Nick helped her, he saw tears glittering in her eyes.

Quinn's baby was so tiny. So helpless.

Nick couldn't tear his gaze away from her. In a few months, God willing, Sierra would hold their baby in her arms.

And if he walked away, he would be doing to his child what Nick's parents had done to him. Abandoning it. Leaving it unprotected.

He couldn't do that. He would never leave a child of his.

SIERRA BIT HER LIP AS she gazed at Maddie and Quinn's baby. She was wrapped in a pink blanket and wore a tiny cap with a pink pom-pom on top. She had a red face and dark blue eyes.

She was gorgeous.

"She's so small," Sierra whispered, her hand creeping to her own belly.

"Seven pounds, six ounces," Quinn announced proudly.

"How's Maddie?" Jen asked.

"Exhausted. Wrung out. Sore." He grinned. "Completely over the moon."

Walker slung his arm over Jen's shoulders as he stared at the baby. Then he kissed his wife, put his hand on her still-flat abdomen and murmured, "Six more months."

Sierra's eyes welled with tears. She wanted that. Wanted what Jen and Walker had, what Maddie and Quinn had found. She had prepared herself for going through pregnancy alone, prepared to be a single mother. She was fine with the choices she'd made.

But seeing Quinn holding his daughter, seeing Walker so happy about Jen's pregnancy, made her ache. She wanted a partner who was just as excited about the baby as she was. A partner who would hold his son or daughter with love and tenderness.

She glanced at Nick, right next to her. He'd been wonderful tonight. He'd stayed with her, tried to reassure her, tried to make her more comfortable. But now his eyes were sad as he looked at the people gathered around Quinn.

When she caught his eye, he murmured, "Scary."

"What is?"

"She's so tiny. So helpless. How do you protect her?"

"I don't know. I guess you learn as you go."

He shoved his hands into his pockets as he watched Quinn and Grace.

Grace was sleeping now, her tiny mouth pursed and her lips twitching. Jen and Walker were cooing over her. Quinn held her securely to his chest.

Surrounded by people, Sierra had never felt so alone in her life.

CHAPTER NINETEEN

NICK SAT IN THE CHAIR next to Sierra's bed, watching her as she slept. His eyes were gritty from lack of sleep and his head ached. They'd had one final ultrasound, and the doctor had told them everything looked good. The spot on the placenta hadn't changed, so it was probably an artifact, whatever the hell that meant.

Sierra had fallen into a deep sleep almost as soon as the doctor walked away. She'd said she wanted Nick here, but he wasn't sure he wanted to stay. Ever since Murphy had brought his baby into the room, Nick had felt a wall between himself and Sierra.

No. It had been there all along. He'd just never noticed it before, because he'd been so busy maintaining his own wall.

Anger rose again, and this time he didn't try to ignore it. She'd risked their child because she had to do everything herself. He'd told her he would try to be a part of her life. He was trying but she still didn't believe in him.

He stood abruptly to leave, and got as far as the door when Sierra said sleepily, "Where are you going?"

"I'm leaving. I'll come back and get you later this morning."

There was a short pause. "I know the chair is uncomfortable," she said.

He turned to face her. "That's not why I'm leaving, Sierra."

"Why, then?" she asked with a puzzled look.

"I'm leaving because I'm pissed off, and I didn't want to have this conversation in the hospital. But maybe it's better if we do."

"What's wrong, Nick?" She lifted herself until she was sitting, propped against the pillows. Dark circles still shadowed her eyes and her hair was falling out of her braid. He was a bastard for doing this now. But he was going to do it anyway.

"You've been telling me for three months that you need me to open up to you, to care about you, to bond with you. To be part of your perfect family. And I've been feeling guilty as hell because I haven't done it. I didn't think I could.

"But I've changed, Sierra. I want this. I want to be with you. I want to make a family with you. Only I realized yesterday that maybe you don't want that, because you haven't let *me* in, either. You don't let anyone in, do you? You want to raise the baby alone, so you can make that perfect family you want so much."

"What are you talking about?" she whispered. She drew the blanket up to her neck.

"Yesterday afternoon, I could have handled that shingle situation for you. Rich would have given them to me, but you wouldn't let me help you. That's just a small thing, but it's a perfect example."

His voice rose, and he closed the door. "You could have lost our baby because you ran after Kyle and fell. Why didn't you ask me to do it?"

She pulled her knees up beneath the blanket, curling into a tight ball. "I told you, I didn't think. I just reacted."

"Exactly. Your first instinct is to do it yourself. To not let anyone in. And that was your first instinct with me, too. I'll admit I was an ass at the beginning. But I've been trying, Sierra." He stared at her. "Have you?"

"I…I…" she stammered. Her throat worked, and she reached for the cup on the table and took a drink. Her hand trembled as she set the cup down, and she gripped the blanket tightly and tucked it beneath her chin.

He wanted to go to her and wrap her in his arms and tell her he didn't mean it. That he was a jerk. But if he did that, it would eat away at him. Now that he'd started, he had to get it out. "At the beginning, I wanted to give you money. It was all I had to give, but I needed to feel as if I was taking some responsibility. That I was doing the right thing. But you wouldn't let me do that, because you didn't want me to be part of your life. Or the baby's."

"You said you couldn't love either of us," she whispered. "I didn't want to hurt my child."

"You didn't even want me to try. You just kept pushing me away."

"I'm not pushing anymore," she said. "I want you to stay."

"Are you sure about that? Are you sure you want the messiness of a relationship, a partner, someone who will expect to have an equal say in how our child is raised? Someone who might argue with you about decisions you make?"

"Yes. I want that."

She blinked hard, several times in a row. Was she going to cry? *Please, God, don't let her cry.*

"I'm not sure you do. You want me to reveal my deepest feelings and secrets, but you haven't been very forthcoming with your own feelings."

She stared at him, tears dripping down her face.

He shoved his hand through his hair and sighed. "Hell, this is why I didn't want to get into this now."

"You've been angry at me since I fell, haven't you?" She sat straighter in the bed. "Was all your concern, your tenderness, your caring real? Or was it just a show to calm me down and make me feel better?"

"What do you think, Sierra?"

She studied his face, her fingers pleating the thin blanket that covered her. "I don't know," she finally said.

He swallowed. "That's honest, at least. When you figure it out, let me know. I'll be back later to pick you up."

Sierra watched Nick walk down the hall. His steps never faltered and he didn't slow down as he disappeared from view.

He was upset she'd run after Kyle. And he was right to be. It had been a stupid thing to do, and almost had horrible consequences. But that didn't mean she was shutting him out in other things, too. She'd invited him into her home; included him in the first ultrasound…. It didn't mean she wanted him to have nothing to do with the baby.

Are you sure, Sierra?

Her mother's voice echoed in her head, asking the question in the calm tone she'd used when her daughter was faced with a decision. It made Sierra squirm.

Nick's behavior when she'd told him she was pregnant had hurt her deeply. But she'd run away before they could discuss it any further. He'd made it clear he was terrified of being a father, but wanted to do what he could. Money was all he had to offer—or so he thought.

And she had refused to take it. Because she didn't want him to be a part of their lives. After losing her parents, she hadn't wanted any uncertainty in her life.

The baby kicked once, then again. Harder. Nick should be here to feel it. He'd been just as worried last night as she had been. She'd seen the truth in his face.

So why had she asked him if it was real? Why hadn't she trusted him?

Nick's words had been hard to hear. Painful. But maybe there was a grain of truth in them.

AT TEN O'CLOCK, NICK walked into the room and stopped a few feet from the bed. He'd changed the bloody clothes he'd been wearing, and must have taken a shower, because his hair was still damp. "How do you feel?" he asked. She couldn't tell what he was thinking.

"Tired," she answered, trying not to let her mouth quiver. "Ready to go home."

"The nurse said the doctor would be looking at the last ultrasound in a few minutes. She's with another patient, but it shouldn't be long."

"I've been thinking about what you said earlier," Sierra began, but Nick raised his hand.

"Not now, okay? I shouldn't have said all that. I was tired, and worried about you and the baby, and it all spewed out. I'm not used to talking about my emotions. Let's leave it alone."

"I'm not going to leave it alone." Anger stirred and swallowed the grief and pain. "You can't just unload on me like that, then say forget about it." Without thinking, she leaned closer to him. "Or didn't you mean it?"

He sank into the chair next to the bed. "I meant it," he said wearily. "But I'm not sure there's anything to discuss. We're both tired, and right now it would be nothing more than 'No, I didn't. Yes, you did.' That wouldn't be productive."

"Productive? Was what you said productive?" Her anger burned brighter, protecting her from the pain. "You couldn't have waited until I was a little less shaky?"

"Maybe I should have, but it was a long night for me, too. I lost every bit of control when I saw you lying on the ground, bleeding." He began to reach for her hand, then sighed. "Hell, Sierra, I've screwed up plenty in the last three months. But at least you always knew where I stood. I always told you what I wanted. Even when I was being a total bastard, I told you the truth."

"And you think I didn't?"

"I'm not sure you knew."

He dropped his hand on the arm of the chair, and she began to reach for it. "I know what I want, Nick. I want you." She curled her fingers into her palm when he didn't reply.

"Last night, I wanted you to stay," she said.

"I know you did. And I wanted to. I thought it would be better if I left. If we both tried to sleep."

"And did you? Sleep?"

"No. Did you?"

"What do you think?"

The silence between them was heavy with unspoken words and regrets. She'd twisted the edge of the sheet into a tight spiral by the time the doctor came into the room, smiling.

"Everything looks good, Sierra. There's no tear in the placenta, no damage to the uterus. You need to take it easy for a few days, but the rest of your pregnancy should proceed uneventfully."

Her throat swelled, but she didn't cry. She'd shed too many tears last night, and she was cried out.

"The nurse will be here in a few minutes with your discharge papers. I need to see you in a week, all right?"

"I'll be there."

The doctor glanced at Nick. "Your partner is welcome, too."

He nodded, but didn't agree to come. Sierra's throat prickled again.

SHE TRIED NOT TO FALL asleep on the way home, but the adrenaline of the past twenty-four hours had drained away, leaving her as limp as a wet dishcloth. She jerked her head up as she felt herself begin to nod off, then her eyes closed again.

"Wake up, Sierra. We're home."

Struggling awake, she opened her eyes and saw Nick hovering over her. "I need to get you upstairs," he said.

She lifted her head and saw the rear of her building. Nick had parked in her assigned spot behind the restaurant. "Okay."

She fumbled for her purse, and Nick took it from her. He helped her out of the car, steadied her as he locked the door, then swept her into his arms.

"I can walk." She looked around. "Where are those crutches they gave me?"

"In the trunk. I'll carry you now and get them later."

Nick stood sideways as he opened first one door, then unlocked and opened the other. She clung to him as he mounted the steps. "I'm too heavy for you to carry. I'll walk up the stairs."

He glanced down at her. "You can't even let me do this? You can't walk up the damn stairs."

He was right. The local anesthetic the doctor had used had worn off hours ago, and her leg throbbed. Every beat of her heart sent a jolt of pain through the muscle, because she hadn't taken the pain medication they gave her. The doctor had assured her it wouldn't hurt the baby, but she hadn't taken any meds during her pregnancy, and she didn't want to start now.

When they reached the top of the stairs, he eased her out of his arms and propped her against the wall. He kept one hand on her hip as he unlocked the door, reached in and turned on the light. He swung her into his arms and carried her to her bedroom, where he laid her on the bed.

"Thanks, Nick," she said as she curled onto her side. Sleep was closing in, and her mind was filled with cotton. "I'm good now."

His fingers circled her ankle as he pulled off one boot, then the other. Something tugged at her hair, and he began to loosen the braid. She remembered him weaving her hair together at the hospital, and she put her hand on his to stop him.

"Leave it," she said, and her voice sounded as if it were coming from far away. "I like it. You did it for me."

His hand stilled on hers, then she felt him touching the long tail of her hair. "Okay. I'm going to pull off the scrub top. Is that all right? You'll be more comfortable if you take it off." He cleared his throat. "Your bra, too. I'll just unhook it. You can take it off yourself."

His hands drifted up her chest, then soft cloth,

smelling of antiseptic, came over her head. He moved to her back, and everything loosened. Then he covered her with a blanket and turned out the lights. Moments later, she was asleep again.

SUNLIGHT STREAMED IN her window, warm and comforting on her face. She opened her eyes to see the curtain fluttering in the lake-scented breeze. The sun was dipping toward the horizon, and her clock said it was three-thirty.

She had fallen asleep after she got home from the hospital. As she flopped onto her back, Sierra touched her abdomen to reassure herself the baby was still there. It fluttered against her hand, and she smiled.

Ignoring the white-hot poker that stabbed into her leg as she rolled to a sitting position, she rested on the side of the bed for a moment. Her bra dangled on one arm, and she frowned. Why would she take a nap like that?

Nick. He'd brought her home. She vaguely remembered him carrying her up the stairs and laying her on the bed. He'd helped her get undressed, even though he was angry at her. Angry and hurt.

Tossing the bra onto the dresser, she sat up on the side of the bed and wriggled until she got the pants off. She stood on one leg as she pulled on an old pair of basketball shorts and a University of Illinois T-shirt. Then she took the crutches Nick had retrieved from the car, and carefully made her way to the bathroom.

She slid the now-ragged braid through her fingers

before she began to unwind it. Nick had done that for her. He had also maneuvered his body between her and the ultrasound screen, in case there was something horrible there.

He'd told her about his childhood to distract her, then stayed with her all night, holding her hand, drying her tears.

Then, when he'd known the baby was going to be all right, he'd erupted in anger over the way she'd treated him.

She'd been too tired to think rationally last night, but they would talk now. They'd straighten everything out.

After tugging the strands of the braid apart, she brushed her hair vigorously, but the kinks from the braid were still there. No matter how long she brushed, they wouldn't go away.

The memory of Nick's tenderness last night wasn't going away, either. Had it been real?

He'd said it was, and that she was the one who wouldn't let *him* in.

She'd begged him to love her. To be part of his child's life. And he'd always refused.

He's been different in the last couple of weeks, the voice that sounded like her mom's reminded her. *But have you given him a chance?*

Sierra thumped toward the kitchen to get a cup of tea, then stopped dead in the hallway.

Nick was sprawled on her couch, wrapped in her mother's multicolored afghan. His bare legs hung over the end, and the blanket angled over one shoulder, exposing a swath of black hair on his chest.

What was he doing here? She took a step toward him, then halted. What was she supposed to do? Let him sleep? Wake him up? Ignore him?

She took another step closer, then another. She'd never seen him sleeping. His aloofness, his cool way of observing the world, was gone. His face was relaxed and appeared much younger.

What had he looked like as a child? As she tried to visualize it, she wondered, for the first time, if she would see Nick's face when she gazed at their child. Would the baby have Nick's eyes? His chin? His nose?

Would she remember the baby's father every time her son or daughter laughed?

If Nick left, how would she bear it?

When she focused on Nick again, his eyes were open. Watching her. "Nick." She swallowed. "You surprised me. What are you doing here?"

He sat up, letting the afghan slip to his lap, and reached for the polo shirt on the floor. It tousled his hair as he pulled it on, and she almost reached out to smooth the heavy waves. She'd never seen him with less than perfectly groomed hair.

"I wasn't going to leave you alone." He picked up his jeans from the floor, tugged them on and let the afghan drop as he stood to button and zip them. She caught a glimpse of dark boxers as he pulled the jeans over his hips.

Once dressed, he studied her, and she became

horribly self-conscious of her own clothing. Her shorts were old and baggy and rode low on her hips beneath the swell of the baby. The T-shirt was flimsy from frequent washings, and since she hadn't bothered with a bra, the thin shirt clinging to her swollen belly and chest wouldn't leave much to his imagination.

"How do you feel?" he asked. His eyes drifted down her body.

Resisting the impulse to cross her arms over herself, she said, "My leg is sore, and I ache all over. But the baby moved, so I don't mind." She took a step backward, and nearly stumbled with the crutches. "Let me go and put some clothes on."

"Don't bother for my sake." His gaze scanned her again, as if he couldn't stop himself. "You look fine."

"I'll be right back."

She glanced in the mirror as she entered her room, and it was just as bad as she'd feared. The shirt could have been painted on, and made it very clear just how big she was. Her breasts were much larger than before she got pregnant, and her nipples were clearly visible beneath the light material.

She closed the door, tore off the T-shirt and put on a bra and her baggiest maternity shirt. She left the shorts on, since her jeans wouldn't fit over the bandage, took a deep breath, then returned to the living room.

Nick was standing at the door. "You have plenty of food in your refrigerator," he said. "I'll swing by before work tomorrow. If you need something before that, you can call me."

"You're leaving?"

"We both have some thinking to do. And I think we need to do it alone. I'm not running away anymore, Sierra. I'll be here for you—and I'll be here for the baby. But you have to decide what *you're* willing to give."

CHAPTER TWENTY

RAIN HIT THE WINDOWS in a steady beat, making the sky gray and turning the streetlights on early. Sierra's tea had gone cold on the end table next to the couch when her doorbell rang. Was it Nick, coming back to tell her that he understood why she'd shut him out?

No. He'd been calm. Sure of himself. He'd told her she wasn't blameless in all of this, either, and his words had been uncomfortable to hear.

Struggling to her feet, she went to the door and opened it. Jen stood at the bottom of the stairs, a rain-spattered cardboard box in her arms.

Sierra pushed the door lock and watched as Jen maneuvered through the door and up the stairs. When she walked in, she said, "Food. I cook when I'm nervous, and I've made a lot of meals in the last couple of days. Okay if I put this away?"

"Uh, sure. Thank you."

She began to follow her into the kitchen, but Jen shook her head. "Sit down. I'll take care of it."

A few minutes later, she carried the empty box into the living room and dropped it by the door. "You want some company?"

"I'd love some." Sierra didn't want to be alone with her misery and the creeping realization that Nick had also been right. "Have a seat."

Jen sank into the chair. "Maddie is coming home tomorrow. I made a bunch of stuff for her, too. It's hard to think about meals when you have a new baby." She rested her hand on her abdomen. "I'll be freezing a lot of meals in the next several months."

Jen drew her legs beneath her and studied Sierra's face. "How are you doing?" she asked softly.

Sierra lifted one shoulder. "I'm okay." She was falling apart and trying hard to hide it.

"Everything okay with the baby?"

"The doctor said it was. No problems with the placenta."

"Then it must be Nick. You look like you're about to cry."

The lump in her throat swelled, and she gazed down at her hands, gripping the afghan in her lap. The same one Nick had used, which now carried his scent. "He's angry because I ran after Kyle Cameron. That's why I fell. I should have let Nick or Mark chase him down, but I wanted to do it myself."

"It's hard, isn't it?" Jen said softly. "To ask for help when you're used to doing things yourself. It's one of the biggest adjustments in a relationship." She leaned forward. "Nick has to figure that out, too."

"I think we will." She wasn't so sure. Nick had been pretty angry. "I don't want to talk about it right now, though. I'll start crying and not stop. Tell me about Kyle. What's going on with him?"

"He's sitting in a cell at the police station. Mark caught up with him and dragged him there, then refused to pay his bail."

"I didn't want it to be Kyle," Sierra said quietly. "I knew Mark would be devastated."

"Apparently, Kyle has a gambling problem. He borrowed money from some scary people in Milwaukee, and they want it back. He was responsible for those pieces of concrete you tripped over, too. He took money to let a construction crew dump them there.

"Mark came by and offered to quit. He even gave us names of other contractors who would do a good job."

"Did you fire him?"

"Of course not." Jen looked surprised that she'd ask. "It wasn't Mark's fault. He wasn't stealing from us."

"What's going to happen with Kyle?"

"I suspect Mark will let him sit in jail for a few days, then bail him out. Walker and I probably won't press charges. We'd rather see him get help. Walker is researching good programs for gambling problems."

"You're very generous," Sierra said slowly.

"Kyle's basically a good kid. Sending him to jail would ruin his life, and we don't want to give up on him."

Like Sierra had given up on Nick. "Thank you, Jen," she said.

"For letting the kid responsible for you falling and hurting yourself off the hook?" Jen smiled.

"No. For making me see something." It had been more than giving up on Nick. Sierra hadn't given him a chance in the first place. From the beginning, she'd been determined to raise her child herself. She'd looked at Nick and rejected him as a father for her child, and his horrified reaction to her pregnancy only made her decision seem right.

"Glad I could help." Jen stood. "Call if you need anything. I'll be right downstairs."

"Thanks, Jen. I will." She rose and hugged her friend, then watched her walk down the stairs.

Alone again, Sierra flopped into the big chair by the window with her mom's afghan and watched the rain sheet down. The street below was empty of people, and the few cars that drove by had their wipers going full speed. Tiny lakes of water were arcing out from the curbs.

"I need you, Mom." Closing her eyes, Sierra curled into a ball. "I need your help."

It's not so difficult, honey. Her mother's voice echoed in her head. *Don't always believe what people say. Trust what they do. You'll be fooled once in a while, but most of the time, you'll see the truth.*

Her mother had spoken those words so many times when Sierra had been hurt by the careless words of friends, or teachers, or colleagues. *Trust what they do.*

"I want what you and Dad had, but I don't know how to get it, and you left before you could tell me. I'm afraid to take Nick at his word. What if I let myself love him, and he leaves?'' The words fell into the silence of the tiny apartment, and there was no answer. How could there be?

As she huddled in the chair, thinking about her parents, the way they'd trusted each other, loved each other, Sierra remembered her mother's journals, sitting on the bookshelf. She had brought them with her to Otter Tail, but hadn't looked at them. Reading them had seemed like an invasion of her mom's privacy, but having them close by was like having a small piece of her mother still with her.

Unwinding the afghan, Sierra retrieved the box of journals from the shelf of the bedroom closet and settled on the couch. A faint hint of her mom's scent drifted up to her as she opened the box.

She trailed her fingers over the stack of brown and black leather notebooks. Then, hand shaking, she picked up the one on top.

SIERRA CLOSED THE LAST journal and replaced it carefully in the box, then stared out into the darkness. It was almost morning. Rain beat against the window, and thunder boomed in the distance. How had she not known?

Her father had had an affair, back when she was a teen. Her parents had come close to divorcing. How could she have been so blind?

Her parents had been desperate to keep the truth from her. Desperate to maintain the facade of a happy family. They had wanted her to be secure. To know she was loved. When they'd all been together, everything had seemed fine.

But her mother had written about arguments behind closed doors, about her and Sierra's father shouting at each other in whispers. Tears that had soaked her pillow. The careful politeness of strangers in front of their daughter.

How had Sierra missed all that?

It had been easy, she realized. She'd been a teenager, consumed with her own life. Her own problems. She'd seen what she wanted to see.

And her parents had been very careful to hide their pain and anguish.

The perfect family, the parents who never fought, never disagreed, had been an elaborate facade. A lie.

Her mother hadn't loved her father during that horrible time—she'd been very clear about that in her journals. Any love she had for him had been destroyed by his affair.

Her parents had been happy the last several years. *Like kids in love again,* her mother had written. It hadn't been easy. But they'd done it. They'd worked at it until they rediscovered their love for each other.

Was that any different than Sierra and Nick, working through their problems? If her parents could find their way through adultery and come out on the other side, happy and in love again, people could get through anything.

If they loved each other enough.

She loved Nick.

He said he wanted to be with her, but she wasn't letting him in. Could she let down all her barriers and take a chance?

Her parents had done it.

Could she?

HER EYES BURNED FROM hours of reading, and she was thirsty. As she pulled a pitcher of water from the refrigerator, Sierra saw a box she didn't recognize on the counter. As she drank, she opened it and peered inside.

From the hospital, it held the jeans they'd cut away from her leg, the green shirt, rusty and stiff with dried blood. She tossed them in the trash.

There was a small, square box of tissues, the ones Nick had used to dry her tears. The tissues were coarse and uncomfortable, but she set the box to one side.

A pair of booties that they'd given her to keep her feet warm in the emergency room.

A copy of the last sonogram, where the baby seemed to be looking right at them.

A battered leather wallet.

It wasn't hers. The smooth leather caressed her fingertips as she slid it open and looked at the driver's license. It was Nick's. He must have taken it out to give the hospital insurance information, then tossed it into the box. She'd make sure he got it back.

She picked it up again. This was snooping. Snooping was wrong. But she wanted to see what he kept in there.

His address. She didn't even know where he lived.

Did he keep pictures of friends? People who were important to him?

Silently apologizing, she opened it up and glanced at his driver's license. He lived on Lake Shore Drive. That wasn't a surprise.

There were no pictures of any kind. Nothing personal. Just a few credit cards and some cash.

Something hard with the bills made it difficult to close the wallet. She tugged it out and examined it—a gray plastic rectangle that looked like a hotel room key.

She turned it over in her fingers and stilled.

It was a room key from the hotel they'd stayed at in Los Angeles.

The number 15 was written in black marker. So was the date: 1-23.

It was the key to her room. The room where he'd helped her undress, put her in the shower, taken care of her.

Held her while she cried.

Made love to her.

She turned the key over, looking at it again, as memories came flooding back. He'd been so gentle. So tender. He'd told her he wouldn't make love with her, wouldn't take advantage that way, but when she'd begged, he'd kissed her. She'd wrapped her arms around him and refused to let go.

And he'd kept the key.

Trust what he does.

She sank onto the kitchen chair. There was only one explanation for why he'd kept this key in his wallet all this time.

Only one thing that made sense.

Clutching the key in her hand, she hurried into the living room and put on her boots. The boots he'd given her. She searched her briefcase frantically, taking a deep breath when she found what she needed. Then, without taking the time to get a jacket or her crutches, she grabbed her keys and headed out the door.

THE LIGHTS OF THE BIDE-A-WEE Motel were dark, except for the No Vacancy sign. She climbed out of the car at the office, not caring that she was getting soaked. She tapped the bell twice, her hands gripping the edge of the counter as she waited. Finally, after what seemed like an eternity, Myrtle opened the door at the back of the office.

"No vacancies," she said. "Sorry."

"Ms. Sanders, it's me. Sierra Clark. I stayed here a while ago. Remember?"

Myrtle's eyes softened. "Yes, I do. Sorry, honey. I'd give you a room if I had one. I'm all filled up tonight, though. There's a wine festival."

"I don't need a room. I need Nick Boone. I know he's staying here. What room is he in, please?"

"I'm not supposed to give out that information," Myrtle said. "Never know who's looking for a person." She rocked back on her heels as she studied Sierra. "You don't look real dangerous, though."

Sierra thought her eyes twinkled, although it was hard to tell in the dim light. "Please, Mrs. Sanders. I need Nick."

Myrtle nodded. "He's in 119. First floor, other side."

"Thank you," Sierra said. She hobbled out to her car and drove to the other side of the building. There were no parking spots close by, so she parked on the far end of the lot and walked through the rain. By the time she got to 119, her hair was soaked and her shirt clung to her skin.

She knocked on the door, listened. Didn't hear a thing, and panic stirred. Had he left? Gone back to Chicago?

She knocked again, harder, in time with the beat of her heart. Finally, she heard a noise inside. Around the edge of the curtain, she saw a light come on. The sound of a chain sliding through its holder, then the door swung open.

Nick stood there in jeans, the top button undone, his chest bare, his hair tousled. His face was drawn and his eyes were weary. He held himself carefully, as if everything hurt.

"Sierra. What are you doing here?" He grabbed a polo shirt and slid it on.

"May I come in, Nick?"

"You want to talk? At this time of night?"

She pushed past him. "This can't wait."

He closed the door behind her. It was impossible to

read the expression on his face. He was the Nick he used to be. Cautious. Guarded. Wary.

Her wet shorts stuck to her legs, and she had to yank at the material to loosen it. Her body wobbled as she lowered herself to the floor and onto one knee, careful of the cut on her leg.

"What are you doing?" he asked. Some of the weariness faded, replaced by concern. "Get up, Sierra. Are you all right?"

"I've never been better." She took his hand and held it tightly. "Nick Boone, will you marry me?"

"What?" His fingers curled around hers. "What are you talking about?"

"Marry me, Nick. Please." She clung to his hand. "You said I was shutting you out, and you were right. I don't want to do that. I love you, Nick."

Her heart compressed when his expression stayed guarded. Had he decided she was too much work?

"Last night, you weren't sure that I was genuinely concerned about you and the baby. Now you want to marry me?"

Shame flushed her cheeks. "I'm sorry. I've been accusing you of not letting anyone get close, but I was just as bad. I used your words to convince myself I was better off alone. I forgot to pay attention to what you did."

"And what did I do that changed your mind?"

"You didn't want to be a father, but you followed me to Otter Tail because you wanted to take responsibility.

You came back when Jen asked you to, even though you didn't want to. Then…last night at the hospital."

She fumbled in her pocket for the room key and held it up. "And this. You took care of me that night. And you kept this."

His cheeks reddened. "How did you get my wallet?"

"You left it in my apartment."

"And you looked through it."

"I'm glad I did. If I hadn't, I wouldn't have known."

"What do you think you know, Sierra?"

"That I might mean something to you. You kept the key."

"And that's what made you propose to me?"

"No. I love you. I want to be with you. And I'm willing to wait for you to figure out how you feel. I finally paid attention to what you did instead of what you said."

"I don't know if I can be the person you want," he said, his voice gruff.

Her throat filled and her heart was pounding so hard she was sure he could hear it. "You already are, Nick. You're exactly the person I want." Her legs trembled, and she held his hand tightly. "Will you please say yes?" she begged. "So I can get up?"

He put his hands on her waist and lifted her almost off her feet. When he set her down, he didn't let her go. "Tell me again why you want to marry me."

"I love you, Nick. I want you in my life forever. And in our child's life."

She touched his face. "I know it's hard for you to trust me. I've had trouble trusting you, too, but I'm going to be completely open with you from now on." She swallowed. "You'll need to be patient with me, but I want you to know me. I want to let you see every corner of my heart. I need you, Nick, and not just for the baby. For me. I love you."

The silence trembled between them. Then Nick cupped her face. His fingers brushed her cheeks, wiping away the tears.

"I've never been in love before, Sierra. It took me a long time to figure it out. Longer to accept it. But I love you. And I love our baby." He caressed her belly gently, then bent to kiss it.

"You're making me sweat here," she said, holding his wrists. "How long are you going to torture me, Boone?"

Finally, he smiled. "I'll marry you, Sierra, and I'll love you forever."

She grabbed his left hand and slipped on the metal nut she'd found in her briefcase. "There. Now it's official. You won't be able to weasel out of it."

"As if I'd try." He rubbed his thumb over the small circle of metal, then brought it to his mouth and kissed it. "You're everything to me."

"Oh, Nick." She threw herself into his arms. "I love you with all my heart. All my soul. Every part of me."

He held her gently as he kissed her. His mouth was

soft on hers, but a river of desire ran through her. She opened her mouth to him, clutched his head in her hands. "Kiss me like you mean it, Nick. Like I've wanted you to kiss me."

"The baby," he murmured, brushing his lips across her cheek and down her throat. "I don't want to hurt the baby."

"Kissing me won't hurt the baby." She closed her eyes and savored the rightness of his mouth on her at last. Of his hands clutching her as if he would never let go.

Nick trailed his hand down her back, up her sides, over her abdomen. Lingered there. "I want you so much, Sierra." He kissed her neck again. "I want to taste you. Kiss every inch of you." He let his mouth trail lower, to the V of her shirt. "I want to watch you when I touch you, when you come apart with me. I want to hear you say my name when I'm inside you."

"Oh, my God. Nick." She was panting, her heart galloping, her body singing with need for him. "Yes. That's what I want, too." She slid her hands to his face, held him as she leaned her forehead against his. "But we can't. It's too soon. The doctor told me to take it easy." Her face heated as she looked at him again. "She didn't say anything about sex, but I'm sure she wouldn't consider that taking it easy."

"Hmm." He trailed his mouth down her neck, lingered over the sensitive hollow above her collarbone. "We'll have to be creative, then." He tugged at her damp shirt. "We should get these wet clothes off you. I don't want you to get a chill."

She was so hot she was afraid she might burst into flames. "Chills would be bad. But I'm not sure getting naked is—"

"I love that you're afraid you can't control yourself." He kissed the tip of her nose. "I guess I'll have to be the strong one."

As he kissed her again, he murmured against her mouth, "How long do we have to wait?"

"We'll ask the doctor when we see her next week," she said, catching her breath as he nibbled her lower lip.

"That's a long time." He nuzzled beneath her ear. "In the meantime, looking is okay, right? And touching?" He tugged gently at her earlobe. "Because I really need to touch you."

CHAPTER TWENTY-ONE

HE UNBUTTONED HER SHIRT slowly, his fingers spreading the material inch by torturous inch, kissing the skin he revealed as he went. By the time he reached the last button and pressed his mouth to her abdomen, she was trembling. She tried to rip the shirt over her head, but he stopped her.

"Let me."

He drew it up slowly, kissing each rib, making her skin jump and burn. After he finally tossed it aside, she put her hands over her breasts. "Ugly bra," she managed to say. "There are no sexy maternity bras."

"You think I care what your bra looks like?" He pried her hands away and trailed his finger along the edge of one cup, down into the valley between them, up the edge of the other.

Shivers ran from her breasts down her abdomen, pooled between her legs. "Nick," she whispered, sliding her hands beneath the polo. He gently pulled them away.

"Not yet." He leaned forward and pressed his mouth between her breasts. His erection slid against her abdomen, and she leaned into him. "I have my list of fantasies I want to get through."

"Maybe we can share fantasies," she said, rubbing against him.

He lifted his head and his eyes glittered. "Oh, yeah," he said. "That sounds like lots of fun. But not this first time. This time, it's all about you."

"That's not fair."

"That's my final offer. Take it or leave it. And first on my list are these sensitive breasts." He cupped both of them in his hands and rubbed his mouth over them. Even through the heavy bra, it made her legs weaken, and she stumbled against him. He drew her onto the bed.

"Since you're self-conscious about this, let's get rid of it," he said, unhooking the bra and drawing it down her arms. He propped himself on one elbow and gazed at her. "You're so beautiful." He traced the blue veins that had become so prominent. "Is this because you're pregnant?"

"Yes." She watched his hands, shivering, desire building inside her.

"Sexy," he said, kissing one of the veins. "Mine."

"Yours," she whispered. He bent and touched his tongue to one nipple, and she cried out.

He froze. "Was that too hard? Did I hurt you?" His breath was warm against the moisture left by his mouth, and she shook her head.

"No," she managed to say. "It's good. Please. Again."

His erection swelled even more against her thigh. He gently suckled, and she began to throb. She could think of nothing but the pleasure building inside her, focus only on what Nick's mouth and hands were doing. When he touched her other nipple at the same time, tension began to coil inside her, and she cried out again. "Nick! Stop! I can't… I'm going to…"

"You're going to what?" he said, swirling his tongue around her, then sucking again. "Tell me," he murmured when she whimpered. "What's going to happen if I don't stop?"

"I'm going to come," she said in a rush. She was so close. She ached for release, wanted him to touch her. She couldn't bear it if he stopped.

"My God," he said. His voice was hoarse. He licked her once more, touched her again, and her climax rolled over her, making her cry out. She clasped his head to her breast until she collapsed, still quivering, against him.

He held her tightly, his mouth pressed to her hair, murmuring soothing words. His erection was hot beneath her, and desire began building again. "That was amazing," she whispered. She tugged his shirt up and brushed her mouth over his chest. His skin burned her mouth, and she pressed tiny sucking kisses over his chest and his rock-hard abdomen.

He sucked in a breath sharply, then eased away from her. "Sierra." He kissed her as he cupped her breast, and she arched helplessly against his palm. "It was the sexiest thing I've ever seen." He nibbled at her lower lip, then soothed it with his tongue, and she shifted restlessly next to him. "Let's do it again."

"No. It's your turn." She reached for the waistband of his jeans, but he drew her hands away.

"I'm not nearly done with you." He sat up and pulled off her jeans, and she felt a flash of self-consciousness again. She wasn't the slim woman he'd seen the last time they'd made love. "I want to look at you." He put both hands on her abdomen, and she shivered. He trailed his fingers over her, as if memorizing her shape. Her size.

"This is beautiful." His hands swept in graceful arcs over her, moving slowly, as if trying to absorb her through his fingers. "I feel as if I'm touching our baby."

The baby moved, as if responding to her father's voice. "Can you feel that?" Sierra shifted his hand to the right spot.

"Yes." He sat up and leaned over her. "Do it again," he whispered, and her heart trembled as she realized he was talking to the baby.

The baby kicked again, and he smiled. "You know who your daddy is, don't you?"

"Nick." Sierra swallowed tears as he bent to kiss her abdomen. "How could you ever think you didn't know how to love me? Or our baby?"

"I didn't, until you taught me," he murmured, his hand resting possessively on the swell of her abdomen. "I watched you, and you showed me how."

She sat and reached for him. "I've wanted this for

so long. Wanted *you*. I'm sorry I was afraid to take a chance. Afraid to trust you."

"We both made mistakes." He drew her close, kissed her, touched her gently. Almost reverently. He smiled against her mouth. "I made a lot more than you, though."

"You're making up for it now." She tugged at his shirt. "And you have way too many clothes on. I'm naked in all my fat pregnantness, and you still have all your clothes on."

"I love your pregnantness." He smoothed his hand over her belly again, then tugged on her panties. "I want to see the rest of you."

"You first," she said, holding on to them.

He watched her as he stripped off his shirt and tossed it to the side, then his jeans. His erection swelled the front of his boxers. "Your turn," he whispered.

She'd been self-conscious about her body. About Nick seeing her this way. But the love in his eyes, the heat, gave her the courage to strip the cotton bikini panties down her legs. She sat in front of him, completely bare. Exposed.

A muscle twitched in his jaw as he gazed at her. He touched the dark red hair at the juncture of her thighs, and she sucked in a breath. "You're the most beautiful woman I've ever seen. I want to touch you everywhere, Sierra. Kiss you everywhere. And next week I'm going to make love with you until neither of us can move."

He shoved his boxers down his legs, then eased her onto the bed when she reached for him. She buried her face in his chest, rubbed her cheek against the soft hair there, and inhaled his scent.

He feathered his hand over the bruises on her stomach. "Do they hurt a lot?"

"They're not too bad. You're making me forget all about them." He slid his hands over her belly again, and when he bent to kiss the bruises, she was suddenly self-conscious. She felt enormous and awkward. Not sexy.

"It must be weird to make love to a pregnant woman." She swallowed as she looked at his dark hair against the pale skin of her belly.

"It will be different." He kissed her again. "But I can't wait. I love you, Sierra. I want to make love with you. I want to know every bit of you. I want to watch you change as you get bigger and bigger with my baby. I love your curves. Your sensitive breasts. Your belly, protecting our child."

"You're going to make me cry," she said, burrowing her fingers into his hair, holding him against her. Against their baby. "You've made me so happy."

"Is that right?" He slipped his fingers lower, stroking her. "I'd rather make you scream."

NICK DIDN'T WANT TO MOVE. He was afraid it was a dream, and he didn't want to wake up. Then Sierra turned her head and whispered, "I love you, Nick." Her breath tickled his ear, and he twitched. Turning his head, he found her mouth and kissed her, a long, slow exploration of her taste and the textures of her mouth.

"I love you, too," he murmured against her lips. "When can we get married?"

"It takes at least a year to plan a wedding," she said, kissing his chin. "Usually more."

"A year!" He jerked away from her. "I'm not waiting a year. The kid will be walking by them. Hell, in a year, he could be my best man."

"That's a great idea. We could put him in a tiny tux, with little patent leather shoes."

He rose up on one elbow. "A year? Tiny tuxes? You're kidding me, right? Tell me you're joking."

"Maybe we should wait until he has a brother or sister. Then they could both be in the wedding."

He heard her giggling, and he flopped back down. "I never knew you had this evil streak," he said.

"I never knew you were so gullible." She nipped at his neck. "This is going to be fun."

He pulled her close to him again. His heart melted at the sight of her twinkling eyes and laughing face. She was his life. His wife, as soon as he could make it happen. "You're forgetting that I have a secret weapon."

"Yeah? What's that?"

"I know your secrets." He lifted her up and took her breast in his mouth. "I know how to make you helpless in seconds," he said, smiling when she squirmed against him.

"You're using my weakness against me," she said.

"What weakness is that?" He laid her on her side

and kissed her again. He would never get tired of kissing her.

"You, Nick." She wrapped her arms around his neck. "You're my weakness."

He smiled, touching her nose with his. "You're my weakness, too. So I guess we're even."

As they held each other's gaze, his heart expanded until it felt too big for his chest. This incredible woman loved him. Wanted to marry him. She was having his child.

They were going to have a perfect life.

EPILOGUE

Christmas Day

SIERRA STOPPED ON THE walkway to admire Jen and Walker's new house, and Nick slipped his arm around her waist. "It's beautiful. A masterpiece."

"We've always worked well together." She smiled at two-month-old Max, sleeping in the crook of his father's arm. "There's the proof. The most perfect baby in the world."

"You're right, of course, but don't say that to Maddie and Quinn. Grace might overhear you."

"It'll be our secret." Sierra kissed her husband and felt the familiar desire rise inside her.

Then the front door opened. "Get in here, you two," Jen called. "No making out on the lawn."

Laughing, they hurried inside out of the cold. Maddie and Quinn were already there, and so were Sam and Delaney and their two kids. Jen cooed over Max and held out her arms. "May I hold him?" She patted her own huge belly and grinned. "I have to practice."

"Sure." Nick handed him over, and Sierra smiled at the reluctance on his face.

"You're going to have to put him down sometime," she whispered. "Sooner or later, he's going to want to crawl. Then walk."

"We're discussing that," Nick said. "He thinks he'd like to be carried everywhere."

Smiling, she pressed a kiss to Nick's mouth. He couldn't bear to be away from his son. The feeling, she was pretty sure, was mutual. Max waved his arms and legs and grinned his huge, sloppy grin whenever he saw his father.

Nick was already planning the employee nursery for when she came back to work.

They dropped off their bottles of wine in the kitchen, where Jen was arranging hors d'oeuvres on plates. "Everyone's in the family room," she said, waving them forward. "Walker will get you a drink."

Jen and Walker's two sons were playing video games, along with Sam and Delaney's nephew Leo. Rennie, their niece, was sitting on the floor with Grace, handing her toys. Grace would toss them away, giggling, and Rennie would bring them back for her.

Maddie leaned forward on the couch to smile at the two children. "She likes you, Rennie."

"I like her, too," the girl assured Maddie. "Her hair is just like mine."

"It is." Maddie smoothed down her daughter's bright red hair, which stood up on her head. She looked like a little red dandelion.

"You're going to have to get one of those for Rennie,

Delaney," Sierra said, watching the two children as she dropped onto a couch.

Delaney leaned against Sam. "Eight months," she said. "Then Rennie will have her own baby to play with."

"Delaney!" Sierra leaped off the couch to embrace her friend. "Congratulations! How are you feeling?"

"I'm great. Couldn't be better."

Jen passed around grilled asparagus wrapped in parmesan cheese, and stuffed mushrooms, then eased onto a chair. "The turkey will be ready in an hour."

Sierra leaned back into the crook of Nick's arm and looked around the room. Conversation and laughter washed over her, punctuated by the shouts of the boys playing video games in the other room and the giggles of the two girls on the floor.

A year ago, she hadn't known any of these people. Last Christmas, she'd spent the day with her mother and father, helping her mom make the turkey and doing the *Times* crossword puzzle with her dad. Her throat swelled with the memory, and she swallowed.

On the night their plane crashed, she'd lost everything most important to her. But out of that pain and grief had come this.

Her husband and their son. These friends, who were becoming like sisters to her. And their growing families.

She and Nick had bought some land to build their dream home near Otter Tail, and they spent as many weekends as possible up here. Their children would all grow up together, playing on the sand, running through the woods, having bonfires on the beach. She'd lost her parents, but she'd found a new family.

"How about a toast?" she said, lifting her glass of wine. "To new beginnings, and new families. And to years of Christmas dinners together."

* * * * *

COMING NEXT MONTH

Available April 12, 2011

HSRCNM0311

REQUEST YOUR FREE BOOKS!
2 FREE NOVELS PLUS 2 FREE GIFTS!

⚜ Harlequin®
Super Romance®

Exciting, emotional, unexpected!

YES! Please send me 2 FREE Harlequin® Superromance® novels and my 2 FREE gifts (gifts are worth about $10). After receiving them, if I don't wish to receive any more books, I can return the shipping statement marked "cancel." If I don't cancel, I will receive 6 brand-new novels every month and be billed just $4.69 per book in the U.S. or $5.24 per book in Canada. That's a saving of at least 15% off the cover price! It's quite a bargain! Shipping and handling is just 50¢ per book in the U.S. and 75¢ per book in Canada.* I understand that accepting the 2 free books and gifts places me under no obligation to buy anything. I can always return a shipment and cancel at any time. Even if I never buy another book, the two free books and gifts are mine to keep forever.

135/336 HDN FC6T

Name _____ (PLEASE PRINT) _____

Address _____ Apt. # _____

City _____ State/Prov. _____ Zip/Postal Code _____

Signature (if under 18, a parent or guardian must sign)

Mail to the **Reader Service:**
IN U.S.A.: P.O. Box 1867, Buffalo, NY 14240-1867
IN CANADA: P.O. Box 609, Fort Erie, Ontario L2A 5X3

Not valid for current subscribers to Harlequin Superromance books.
**Are you a current subscriber to Harlequin Superromance books
and want to receive the larger-print edition?
Call 1-800-873-8635 or visit www.ReaderService.com.**

* Terms and prices subject to change without notice. Prices do not include applicable taxes. Sales tax applicable in N.Y. Canadian residents will be charged applicable taxes. Offer not valid in Quebec. This offer is limited to one order per household. All orders subject to credit approval. Credit or debit balances in a customer's account(s) may be offset by any other outstanding balance owed by or to the customer. Please allow 4 to 6 weeks for delivery. Offer available while quantities last.

Your Privacy—The Reader Service is committed to protecting your privacy. Our Privacy Policy is available online at www.ReaderService.com or upon request from the Reader Service.

We make a portion of our mailing list available to reputable third parties that offer products we believe may interest you. If you prefer that we not exchange your name with third parties, or if you wish to clarify or modify your communication preferences, please visit us at www.ReaderService.com/consumerschoice or write to us at Reader Service Preference Service, P.O. Box 9062, Buffalo, NY 14269. Include your complete name and address.

HSR11

Selene wanted nothing to do with the father of her son, Alex; but Aristedes had other plans...that included them.

Read on for an sneak peek from
THE SARANTOS SECRET BABY by Olivia Gates,
available April 2011, only from Harlequin Desire.

"You were right to turn my marriage offer down," Aristedes said.

And Selene found her voice at last, found the words that would not betray the blow he'd dealt her. "Thanks for letting me know. You didn't have to come all the way here, though. You could have just let it go. I left yesterday with the understanding that this case is closed."

Before the hot needles behind her eyes could dissolve into an unforgivable display of stupidity and weakness, she began to close the door.

The door stopped against an immovable object. His flat palm.

"I can't accept that." His voice was low, leashed.

What did her tormentor mean now? Was he ending one game only to start another?

She raised eyes as bruised as her self-respect to his, found nothing there but solemnity and determination.

Before she could voice her confusion, he elaborated. "I never let anything go unless I'm certain it's unworkable. I realize I made you an unworkable offer, and that's why I'm withdrawing it. I'm here to offer something else. A workability study."

She leaned against the door, thankful for its support and partial shield. "Your son and I are not a business venture you can test for feasibility."

His gaze grew deeper, made her feel as if he was trying to delve into her mind, take control of it. "It's actually the other way around. I'm the one who would be tested."

She shook her head. "Why bother? I know—and *you* know—you're not workable. Not with me."

His spectacular eyebrows lowered over eyes she felt were emitting silver hypnosis. "You're right again. Neither you nor I have any reason to believe that isn't the truth. The only truth. It might be best for both you and Alex to never hear from me again, to forget I exist. But then again, maybe not. I'm only asking for the chance for both of us to find out for certain. You believe I'm unworkable in any personal relationship. I've lived my life based on that belief about myself. I never really had reason to question it. But I have one now. In fact, I have two."

Find out what happens in
THE SARANTOS SECRET BABY by Olivia Gates,
available April 2011, only from Harlequin Desire.

SPECIAL EDITION

Life, Love, Family and Top Authors!

In April, Harlequin Special Edition features
four *USA TODAY* bestselling authors!

FORTUNE'S JUST DESSERTS
by MARIE FERRARELLA

Follow the latest drama featuring the ever-powerful
and passionate Fortune family.

YOURS, MINE & OURS
by JENNIFER GREEN

Life can't get any more chaotic for Amanda Scott.
Divorced and a single mom, Amanda had given up on
the knight-in-shining-armor fairy tale until a friendship
with Mike becomes something a little more....

THE BRIDE PLAN (*SECOND-CHANCE BRIDAL* MINISERIES)
by KASEY MICHAELS

Finding love and second chances for others is
second nature for bridal-shop owner Chessie.
But will *she* finally get her second chance?

THE RANCHER'S DANCE
by ALLISON LEIGH

Return to the Double C Ranch this month—where love, loss
and new beginnings set the stage for Allison Leigh's latest title.

*Look for these titles and others in April 2011
from Harlequin Special Edition, wherever books are sold.*

A Romance FOR EVERY MOOD™

www.eHarlequin.com

SEUSA0411

MARGARET WAY

In the Australian Billionaire's Arms

Handsome billionaire David Wainwright isn't about to let his favorite uncle be taken for all he's worth by mysterious and undeniably attractive florist Sonya Erickson.

But David soon discovers that Sonya's no greedy gold digger. And as sparks sizzle between them, will the rugged Australian embrace the secrets of her past so they can have a chance at a future together?

Don't miss this incredible new tale,
available in April 2011
wherever books are sold!